D0209421

Sweet MADNESS

Trisha Leaver *and* Lindsay Currie

MeritPress | *fw*

Published by
Merit Press
an imprint of F+W Media, Inc.
10151 Carver Road, Suite 200
Blue Ash, OH 45242. U.S.A.
www.meritpressbooks.com

ISBN 10: 1-4405-8894-5
ISBN 13: 978-1-4405-8894-5
eISBN 10: 1-4405-8895-3
eISBN 13: 978-1-4405-8895-2

Printed in the United States of America.

10   9   8   7   6   5   4   3   2   1

Cover design by Frank Rivera.
Cover images © Shutterstock.com/Raisa Kanareva; apostrophe/123RF.

This book is available at quantity discounts for bulk purchases.
For information, please call 1-800-289-0963.

Dedication

Trisha: For LuLu
Lindsay: To my family. I love you with all my heart.

Acknowledgments

Trisha:

This book would not exist if it weren't for the support and encouragement of countless people. My agent, Kevan Lyon, whose dedication and unwavering support makes all things possible in my writing world.

My editor, Jacquelyn Mitchard, who fell in love with Bridget Sullivan's story from page one and worked tirelessly to make it shine. The entire Merit Press team: Bethany Carland-Adams for fielding countless e-mails (I promise I won't send any more), Frank Rivera for designing the perfect cover, and MT Cozzola, whose mad copyediting skills amaze me.

Kate Conway, Hillary Monahan, and Eva Schegulla for being grounding forces throughout this entire process. My amazing CPs who read countless versions of this manuscript, and my coauthor Lindsay Currie for taking this journey with me.

To my family who has endured this crazy writing obsession of mine with grace and dignity, not once complaining that their dinner was late or their socks were mismatched. And most importantly, my amazingly patient husband, Brian, whose quick wit always keeps me laughing.

Lindsay:

As always, I'd like to thank my husband, John, and my kiddos, Rob, Ben, and Ella for their support while *Sweet Madness* was being written. Their words of encouragement and infinite patience are the reason I'm able to do what I love, and for that I owe them eternally.

I'd also like to thank my agent, Kathleen Rushall, for her constant support. Kathleen—you're amazing. Thank you, thank you, thank you!

Huge thanks to Jacquelyn Mitchard for falling in love with Bridget's story and helping to bring it to the shelves. And thank you to the entire Merit Press team for months and months of hard work!

Last but not least, I'd like to thank Trisha Leaver, for taking this journey through Fall River, circa 1800s, with me. You're the best!

Epigraph

Lizzie Borden took an axe

And gave her mother forty whacks.

When she saw what she had done,

She gave her father forty-one.

Chapter 1

I made my way down the back stairs, excited and nervous at the same time. It had been a few weeks since I'd last seen Liam, and given the extensive list of chores Mrs. Borden had scribbled down last night, it would be a while before the opportunity presented itself again.

It was the dreadful heat I had to thank for this small reprieve. It had Mrs. Borden confined to her room most days, completely incapacitated and unable to properly supervise my work. She still found the time to handwrite me a list of errands to run and household tasks to complete, but as unwell as she was, she seemed content to overlook the smaller details of my employment.

I'd run into Mr. Borden earlier that morning. He'd inquired about my day, more specifically what meals I had planned. It's not that he was looking for something fancy, rather he wanted to inform me that there was plenty left over from last night's supper to make a stew. I nodded and tossed the nearly meatless mutton bone into a pot of water, before asking for permission to spend the day down by the river with my friends. He waved his hand dismissively, as if what I did with my free time was of little interest to him.

Lizzie was my main concern. She'd become nosy lately, constantly at my side, constantly trying to help. It was odd at first—her obvious affection for me—but the more time I spent with her, the easier it became to understand. Lizzie Borden was lonely. A burden to her father and a nuisance in a house that thrived on thriftiness and obedience. She had no one but me to keep her company. Lizzie wasn't meddling, rather looking for a friend, a confidant. And right now, that person happened to be me.

Lizzie had left early that morning to teach Sunday school, then tend to her charity work at the Fruit and Flower Mission. She'd be home briefly for her midday meal, but by then I would be gone.

A weighty sigh drew my attention to the parlor. I silently made my way to the front room, fearing it was Lizzie, praying it was Mr. Borden grumbling over some unexpected expense at his Swansea farm. Mr. Borden I could pacify with a simple, "sorry to disturb you, sir." But Lizzie . . . she'd ask questions.

I thought about ignoring whoever it was and simply leaving through the back door, but the sigh came again, louder and drawn out as if someone were subtly announcing their presence. Lizzie.

"I thought you were visiting with Alice after Sunday worship," I said. Alice Russell was Lizzie's one friend besides me, the only other woman in Fall River Lizzie confided in. And it was days like today I was grateful for their friendship; it gave me a much-needed reprieve from Lizzie . . . from this house.

She shook her head rather than answer, her eyes scanning a letter I could've sworn was addressed to her father.

"I set dinner on the cookstove; it won't be ready for a few hours, but there is some bread and tea in the kitchen if you are hungry," I said, hoping the hunched set of her shoulders and the hollow look in her eyes were due to nothing more than the heat and a bit of hunger.

"In a bit," she said. "Alice is feeling ill, and my own dear sister, Emma, has gone to Fairhaven. I find myself with very little to do. Perhaps I could help you with your chores."

I didn't miss the spark of hope that lifted her last words. It wasn't the first time she'd offered to help, and more often than not I enjoyed her friendly conversation as I hung clothes on the line or emptied the ash bin in the cellar.

"I did most of my chores this morning before the heat became unbearable," I replied.

Lizzie looked up, her eyes fixing on the drawstring purse I had cinched around my wrist. "Where are you going, then?"

"Errands," I lied, then bowed my head and sent up a quick prayer for forgiveness.

She laughed and carefully resealed the letter she was reading before placing it back on the table in the entryway. "Come now, Bridget, do I not deserve the truth?"

On most things, yes, but not this. I don't know why I hid Liam from her, why I would talk freely with Lizzie about my home back in Ireland, my sister Cara and the gossip that shrouded her very existence, but became close-lipped at the mere mention of Liam. Perhaps it was because he was the one thing in Fall River that belonged solely to me, the one thing the Borden family and their wealth couldn't touch.

"I'm not my father," Lizzie added when I remained silent. "I will not begrudge you time with your friend. Liam, is it?"

I searched my memory for any instance when I had spoken of him by name or made any reference to having a male friend, knowing full well I hadn't. "I truly have errands to run, Lizzie. I'd ask you to join me, but I know how the heat disagrees with you."

When she didn't argue, I made my way out the front door, half-expecting her to follow or, at the very least, voice her displeasure over the situation. But she didn't, and that had me even more on edge. It wasn't like Lizzie to set aside her curiosity that easily.

I purposely took a roundabout way to Corky Row, making several unnecessary turns that did nothing more than loop me back to Second Street. But no matter how many times I changed direction, the sturdy and purposeful click of boots against pavement followed me. It wasn't until I rounded the corner to Liam's street that I gave in to my nervous discontent and hazarded a peek over my shoulder. It wouldn't be the first time Lizzie had followed me, but usually she made her presence known by calling out my name.

The street behind me was nearly empty—a few beggar children and some maids hurrying to and from work—but no plainly dressed woman of stature. No Lizzie.

A flare of apprehension quickened my steps. I sought out an alleyway to duck into and concealed myself in the darkness until whoever was following me passed. I knew it was ridiculous. I'd told myself half a dozen times I was being overly suspicious, that my guilt about lying to Lizzie in the first place was getting the better of me. But no logical explanation, no amount of self-condemnation could stop the way I felt. It was that sensation of eyes on you when there shouldn't be that made me believe I wasn't alone.

I stepped behind an abandoned fruit cart, crouched down, and watched as a shadow appeared at the mouth of the alley. *Lizzie.* She paused, her eyes skittering across the darkened corridor as if debating whether I was foolish enough to risk my welfare with the vagrants who called these rat-infested passageways home. With a brisk nod of her head, she walked away, probably assuming I had more sense.

I counted to fifty, then eased my way out from behind the cart, slowly making my way back out to the cobblestone street. Half-hidden in the shadows, I scanned first to my left and then to my right, but she wasn't there. It was as if she had vanished, as if her appearance at the end of the alleyway was nothing more than my conscience-stricken imagination chastising me for lying. But unlike Lizzie, I wasn't prone to fits of fugue. I didn't subscribe to the belief that the voices that plagued her were whispered from beyond, were the voices of those drawn into the Borden curse.

What I saw and the uneasiness I felt were real. I was being followed, silently stalked by my own friend. And she was still there, carefully hidden out of sight. Lizzie wouldn't sulk back home and occupy her time by reading her father's mail or pawing through her stepmother's belongings. No, she'd circle these streets until she found me.

Chapter 2

I sat down on the damp grass and watched Liam show the O'Connor boy how to catch small fish with his bare hands. Liam had been at it for nearly an hour and still had no fish to show for his efforts. But he looked happy, more relaxed than I'd seen him in weeks.

Today was the first day in nearly a month I'd seen Liam. I saw him most evenings, but it was a rare occasion that we actually got to see each other by the light of day. He worked six days a week at the Borden Mill. It wasn't owned by the same Borden family I worked for, but that didn't matter. Seemed like all the wealthy in Fall River could claim some distant relation to each other.

He'd also recently picked up some extra shifts at the mill. It was less about the money and more about covering for his friend Peter Bence. Peter had fallen ill and Mr. Furlong, the mill manager, was threatening to replace him. Liam and what few friends Peter had were doing their best to help him. But even with the extra hours, Liam still struggled to make the rent *and* set money aside for us. He'd been rooming in a tiny, mill-owned tenement house with his five brothers since the day he stepped foot in Fall River four years ago and lately, it seemed like that's where he'd stay.

To my left, the mills stood in all of their bleak, ugly glory. Even running at half-capacity, the smoke billowing from their stone chimneys filled the air with a haze so thick it dampened out the afternoon sun. Tomorrow, when the Lord's Day had passed, the smoke from those stacks would consume the air again, and everyone who lived within a few blocks of those mills would struggle to breathe.

Drops of cold water pulled me from my observations, and I looked up to see Liam's smiling face above me. "Dreaming about me, love?" he asked.

I laughed. He was soaking wet, his cotton shirt clinging to his upper body and his trousers rolled up nearly to his knees. I hadn't been thinking about him at that moment, but there weren't many days that I didn't use the thought of Liam as my escape.

"Perhaps," I said, hoping he knew without a doubt that all of my dreams revolved around him. "I suppose you'll never know, though, now that you've gone and interrupted me."

"That sounds like a challenge, lass. Not a challenge you'd win, either," he said with a laugh.

Easing away from him, I shook my head at the smirk forming on Liam's lips. He knew to keep his hands to himself in public, but that didn't mean he was above teasing me a bit. "I see you caught yourself some dinner, Thomas," I said, motioning to the tiny fish he held.

The O'Connor boy was completely dry and proudly displaying a fish not even worthy of a pan. His parents weren't anywhere to be seen, but that wasn't unusual. His da frequently took the less desirable Sunday shifts for the extra money and his mother . . . well, she was probably home, tending to her newborn son, the seventh sibling to be born in as many years.

Thomas smiled and held the fish up higher. "Liam helped."

Judging from the quality of Liam's clothes, I had no doubt about that. Liam hadn't simply helped. He had dived in headfirst to guddle the tiny fish.

The river was getting crowded, wealthy families and immigrants alike seeking the cool breeze that floated off the water. I pulled the brim of my hat down lower over my brow and scanned the bank for Lizzie. I'd been looking for her since Liam and I arrived nearly an hour ago, thought I'd caught a glimpse of her a time or two. But each time I stood to confront her, the light would change and what I'd assumed was Lizzie turned out to be nothing more than a shadow.

My thoughts drifted back to the Borden house, and I wondered if the noontime meal I'd left simmering in the pot had met with Mr. Borden's approval. The butcher was closed and the ice delivery wasn't scheduled until tomorrow, so I'd had to make do with what I had. Unfortunately, that was day-old mutton and bread.

"Mr. Borden gave you the entire day off, no?" Liam asked as he stretched out next to me on the grass. His hand drifted lazy circles over the sleeve of my dress, and I smiled, dreaming of a future where these quiet moments weren't so few and far between. I reached out and let my hand rest on top of his. He stilled for a moment to squeeze it, then laced his fingers through mine. It wasn't the most intimate gesture, but it was still nice. Calming.

I nodded. "I left their meals on the cookstove. Doubt they'll have need of me at all today."

"Does she know you are here? Is that why your eyes keep drifting to the comings and goings of the people around us? Are you looking for her?"

I didn't bother to question how Liam knew what I was thinking. We'd had this discussion countless times in the past few months. He thought I was too involved with Lizzie's life, or rather the other way around—that she'd taken an unnatural interest in mine. He said it wasn't right for the daughter of my employer to be so meddling, that what I did or where I went on my own time was none of her concern.

"I'm not," I lied. "I just want to make sure I have time to fix you and your brothers a proper meal before I have to leave, 'tis all."

His crooked smile told me he wasn't buying my excuse, but he played along anyway. "It looks like it'll just be me," he said, tilting his head towards the bank of the river. "Doubt we'll be seeing much of my brothers 'til morning."

I didn't need to follow his line of sight to guess at what he was implying. All six of the Higgins boys, Liam included, were handsome. Blue eyes and blond hair, with smiles that could part a girl from her corset in mere minutes. But they were stable too, loyal to a fault and hardworking. That made them promising to the young and widowed alike.

My eyes skirted over his other brothers before settling on Seamus. He was the youngest, seventeen like me, and full of life. He was the one I knew best, the one who Liam tended to spend all of his time with. Call it duty, but Liam had dragged Seamus over here when he was barely thirteen, promising his mother that he'd give him a better life. I don't know if this life was better, but Seamus seemed happy. Liam made sure of that.

"That a new girl?" I asked, motioning towards the blanket Seamus was lounging on. I hadn't seen her before, not at the brothers' flat, not at any of the stores I frequented on my daily errands.

"Doubt it matters. It's Minnie he's got his heart set on," Liam said, and I shook my head. Lucky for Seamus, my best friend felt the same way about him. Minnie would follow Seamus's lead no matter how impulsive or imprudent his ideas might be.

"Do I need to worry about you too?" I joked.

Liam laughed then leaned in and gently tucked a loose strand of hair back into my braid.

"Nope. In another year, I'll have saved enough to get us a real home," he said as he pulled back. "Give you my name and start a family."

"Another year," I whispered as I stared across the river to Swansea. All I had to do was survive the smothering tension of the Borden house for one more year, then I could start living, finally be able to claim the life I'd intended when I first came to America.

Chapter 3

"You sure you can't stay out a bit longer?" Liam asked as he wound his arms around my waist and rested his chin on top of my head. The smell of the river lingered on his skin, reminding me of our afternoon together, an afternoon that had ended with me, Liam, and Seamus sitting around their kitchen table, smiling as we recalled the simplicity of life back in Ireland. I'd have given anything for every day to be like this one—calm and filled with laughter.

I tilted my head upwards and gave him a quick kiss, taking a moment to savor the feeling of his lips on mine. I had no idea if I'd see him tomorrow or even the day after that, but I was determined to make the most of the few minutes we had left.

I remembered the day I'd met Liam. I'd been here no more than two weeks and was working for the Remingtons up on the Hill. I wandered down to St. Patrick's in hopes of finding a familiar face from County Clare back home or the SS *Republic*.

Liam was there, tending to a crack in the church's front walk as he hummed a tune I hadn't heard since the day I left Ireland. That tune, that silly folk song, did me in, and I slumped down right there on the sidewalk and wished myself back home.

"Why the tears, lass?"

I ran the back of my hand across my eyes and looked up, saw his smiling blue eyes staring down at me, daring me to answer.

When I didn't, he tossed his trowel aside and stooped down next to me, forcing me to meet his stare.

"Surely my singing ain't that awful." He did his best to look wounded, and I couldn't help but giggle. He looked more like a sulking child than a grown man trying to make conversation with a pretty girl.

"Your singing is fine, sir."

He laughed then, a full bellow that had everybody around us turning their heads. "I ain't ever been anyone's sir, lass, and I reckon I never will be. Name's Liam. Liam Higgins."

"Bridget Sullivan," I replied.

He extended his hand, and I took it, glad for once to see a smiling face. Up on the Hill, people were polite, courteous *how do you do's* greeted me as I passed through town. But nobody ever smiled like they meant it, asked me how I was faring, or invited me to talk. 'Til Liam.

"So if it ain't my singing, then what has a beautiful lass like you crying?"

"It's silly. It's . . . my mum used to sing me that song."

And Mum hadn't sung it to me so much as to my sister Cara. It was the one thing that seemed to calm my baby sister when she was out of sorts, when the world around her became too confusing for her to bear.

"Aye, so you'd be missing home," Liam said, and I nodded. "How long you been here?"

"Two weeks," I said not bothering to mention the few months I'd spent in Newport with my cousin Harry. In my mind, that didn't count. I was with kin there. Here, I was on my own. Completely alone.

"It'll get easier, you'll see," he said as he stood up and motioned for me to do the same. "So tell me Bridget, what do you know about laying bricks?"

I shook my head. I could shear a sheep and make a stew out of nothing but a mutton bone and some potatoes, but when it came to men's trades, I was lost. "Nothing."

"Good, me neither, but the lad who usually does this is home tending to his ailing wife, so Father asked me to do it. He assured me the Holy Spirit would guide my unskilled hands." Liam paused and rolled his eyes, muttering something under his breath about wasting the Good Lord's time. "I could sure use some company while I try and figure it out, if you've got the time."

Time was one thing I had. And almost two years later, I was still eking out every spare second I could find to spend with him.

"Bridget?" Liam snapped his fingers in front of my face, pulling me from my memory and back to the present, to a world where he was still my center. "You okay, love?"

I nodded and sighed. We'd been standing in the shadows on the edge of Second Street for the last ten minutes, but I had yet to take one step in the direction of my employer's house. I didn't want to, didn't want to leave Liam just so I could be drawn back into the madness that seemed to surround the Borden house. The madness that seemed to surround Lizzie herself.

"How long until you think we'll have enough to bring Cara over and get our own place?" I asked.

Liam turned me in his arms, his eyes speaking the truth his words never would. "Soon, Bridget."

Soon could mean years here in Fall River. Years of scraping by only to see what money you'd managed to save vanish as one of your loved ones fell sick and you were forced to beg, borrow, even steal what you could to buy medicine.

"I know my sister is not your burden to carry—"

"Aye, that's where you are wrong, lass. Your burdens are mine to bear."

He'd said that a thousand times before, thought nothing of bringing Cara here when I'd first told him my plan. But he hadn't met her, had no idea exactly how bad off my sister really was.

My baby sister was "touched in the head" or so our county doctor claimed. She hadn't always been so. She used to run around, laughing and squealing as she rolled a lopsided hoop across the field as I tended to my chores. It was annoying then. Now, it hurt to recall.

I was supposed to be watching her that day. Mum had fallen ill and was tied to the bed, delirious with fever. I was tending to the wash, airing out what I could in the hopes that nobody else took sick. I'd long since sent Cara down to the loch to refill the pail, thinking nothing of the amount of time she'd been gone.

That's where I'd gone wrong.

No one knew how long she'd been under the water that day; most were amazed she even survived. She lived all right, but Cara never was the same after that. She used to forget how to do the simplest things and was prone to violent shakes, ones that left her unconscious on the floor, curled into her own fluids. Even during the good spells, she was off, said things she shouldn't and laughed at the dead air.

Mum did her best to care for her, but each night, when the house stilled with sleep and she thought no one was listening, her whispered words would fill the house. She'd curse me for not watching my sister better, then beg God to take Cara, save her from a life that would be unyielding and cruel.

Now I made my own silent vow each night, one that brought Cara here to America. One that had me tied to this house and the extra ten cents a week Mr. Borden paid me over my previous employer. If that meant staying at the Borden house and looking the other way when Lizzie did or said something odd or when she and her father fought so loudly that the house shook with their anger, then so be it. I could withstand the dark corners of the Borden house, its shadows and flickers of light that bled from one room to the next, if it meant keeping Cara cared for.

"When the time comes, I want to go get Cara myself. I don't think she could handle the trip on her own."

Liam nodded. It'd mean a bit more saving, but it was worth it. "I presumed you would, love."

I took a step out onto the street and turned to look back at Liam, committing every second of this day to memory so that I could recall it later on as I lay in bed, listening to the house settling into stillness.

Liam smiled and took a step towards me, misreading my hesitation for fear. "I can walk you to the door and introduce myself to Mr. Borden so he knows you're spoken for, that you have someone who'd stop at nothing to see you safe."

"Can't," I said, not bothering to give an explanation. Liam already knew the reason why. He made that same offer every time he walked me home, the same sparkle of hope that I'd say yes never dwindling.

Liam's original fascination with Lizzie and the solitary life the Bordens lived had quickly dissipated as I told him about the discord in the house, the days . . . the months Mrs. Borden could go without so much as speaking a word in my direction. The loud disagreements between Lizzie and her father that would rage for hours. And the sounds. The creaking of floorboards. The perpetual chiming of the clock in the parlor. The sudden drafts of air that seeped in from the old windows. Even the wallpaper in my bedroom peeled in sheets with the rise and fall of the temperature, clinging briefly to the cracking plaster before dropping off like bits of drying skin. No matter how much I cleaned, no matter how often I dusted the windowsills or scrubbed the floorboards, it never felt better. Never felt right.

"Let me walk you to the front gate at least, make sure you get in safely." Liam's request didn't stem from curiosity, rather his concern for me.

I shook my head. Mr. Borden had made it very clear he wanted no male suitors darkening his door. He'd gone as far as to make it a non-negotiable condition of my employment. "I'll be fine," I said.

Liam's expression softened and he ran a hand down my cheek. "You have to be patient. I'll get you out of that house, out of Fall River. You have my word."

As people who didn't have much to give, our word meant everything. "I know," I said and squeezed his hand.

The night around us was black and silent, every tiny wisp of a sound making me nearly jump out of my skin. "I'd better get going; it's certainly midnight by now."

"Aye, that it is." Liam dropped one more quick kiss to my cheek, then stepped back into the shadows. I knew him too well, though. He wasn't going anywhere. He'd stay hidden there and watch until I made it safely inside, until the click of the locks on the door drifted through the breeze and the lantern I carried to my room faded into darkness.

Chapter 4

I crossed myself, asking God for strength—or rather courage—before I knocked on Lizzie's bedroom door. She'd been holed up in there all morning, had told her stepmother, Abigail, she'd eat after everyone had gone about their day. Mrs. Borden had speculated that perhaps Lizzie was falling ill, that the heat blanketing Fall River these past few days was causing Lizzie some trouble. I doubted Lizzie's peculiar behavior had anything to do with the heat and everything to do with me.

"I know you are in there, Lizzie," I said as I knocked again. I wasn't concerned about drawing anyone's attention with my raised voice. Andrew Borden was out tending to his morning business, and his wife was visiting her sisters across town.

"I shall get the key," I threatened, knowing full well the door wasn't locked. I'd tested the handle earlier, and it twisted easily in my hand.

I went to knock again, to pound on the wood for a third time, when she opened the door and caught my fisted hand. "Bridget Sullivan," Lizzie said, her free hand melded to her hip as she glared at me. "Why on earth did you lie to me?"

"I didn't lie," I said and took a step back. I'd seen Lizzie angry plenty of times, but until then, her anger had never once been directed at me.

"Really? Because I spoke with Father and he said he'd given you the day off, something about spending time down by the river with your friends."

I hadn't done anything wrong. I'd finished my chores, left the evening meal simmering on the cookstove, and sought my employer's permission before I left. The only thing I was guilty of was wanting to spend time with my friends . . . time away from Lizzie.

"Yes, I did see my friends," I said.

"So why didn't you tell me that yesterday? Why don't you trust me enough to speak the truth? Do you honestly think I would keep you from your friends?"

No, but knowing her, she'd insist on coming along.

I dug my hand into my apron pocket and pulled out a fresh spool of thread. Mrs. Borden had left me a generous pile of mending, and I didn't have nearly enough black thread to let her dress out, never mind stitch the tiny hole in Mr. Borden's trousers. "Besides, I stopped by Minnie's. Your father asked me to mend his suit coat, and we were out of black thread. Minnie kindly gave me hers. So, it wasn't truly a lie."

Lizzie took the thread from my hand and tossed it onto her bed. "I don't understand why Abigail can't do her own mending. It's not like I have anybody around here to do mine."

I went to argue, to tell her that I was more than happy to tend to her clothes, that it was in fact *my job*. But all that would do was draw her into an argument that had nothing at all to do with what I actually wanted to know.

"Why were you following me?" I asked. She had the presence of mind to look offended, inciting me even more. "And don't even tell me you weren't. I saw you at the end of the alley, looking for me."

She grabbed me by the arm and yanked me into her room, shutting and locking the door behind us before motioning for me to sit. I shook my head and planted my hands on my hips, mocking her earlier stance. I didn't want to sit down and listen to her spin a tale. I wanted the truth. Now.

"You followed me all the way to Liam's flat, and I want to know why."

"I didn't follow you anywhere." Her answer was so plainly spoken that for a second I thought it was the truth. "I was here all day doing the mending," she continued, her arm sweeping out towards her black dress and the needle sticking out from the fabric. Beside it on the bed were a pair of Mr. Borden's trousers and an old corset of Lizzie's I'd deemed beyond repair.

I quickly retraced the route in my head, clearly remembering being followed. The distant sound of footsteps, the eerie sensation of being watched, even the shadow of her face at the end of the alley.

May the Virgin Mother keep me safe, I muttered silently to myself. Surely, I hadn't imagined it; this house couldn't be driving me as mad as Lizzie. Then again, it wouldn't be the first time my mind had played tricks on me. There were the tiny voices I heard in the dead of night, the creaking of the floorboards when not a soul but myself was awake. The whispers that permeated my dreams. Even the hushed sounds Mrs. Borden made while she slept carried a sinister tone.

Chapter 5

I paused by the cookstove and listened, the soft clicking of Mr. Deen's footsteps indicating the ice was finally here. Wiping my hands on my apron, I put the bread I was kneading aside and hurried to the back door, thrilled to finally be able to refrigerate leftovers. Mr. Borden had been cheaper than usual with ice lately, and we'd gotten down to nothing but moldy water in the icebox more than two days ago.

I'd just finished thanking Mr. Deen when I heard the front door being unlocked. I glanced at the clock, confused. Even if Mrs. Borden were up, there was no way she'd have left the house without first taking her morning meal. That was the one thing that woman never missed and always complained about—her meals.

I'd been awake and milling around since six. And Mr. Borden . . . well, I'd have heard him going. He would've made a big production of placing the keys to his and Mrs. Borden's room on the mantel in the sitting room, silently daring Lizzie or me to touch them. Mrs. Borden was still asleep; I'd heard her snoring as I passed their room, so that left only—

The front door swung open with a fury, hitting the wall behind it with such force that it left a noticeable nick in the wallpaper. Lizzie burst in, a bundle tucked beneath her arm and a deep flush to her cheeks. The bottom of her skirt was soaked, leaving a line of muddy water behind as it dragged across the hardwood floor.

"Lizzie!" I breathed out, glancing at the stairwell in the hopes that no one but me had heard her come in. The last thing I wanted today was to deal with Mr. Borden's anger. He'd berate Lizzie with questions as to where she could possibly go at this God-awful hour, only to have her fall into one of her fits again. He'd yell and then go his own way, tending to his morning errands while leaving me to deal with a distraught Lizzie in a stone-silent house.

"What in the world are you doing? Where are you coming from?" I asked.

I handed her a dry dishtowel and reached for the already warmed kettle. No matter how hot and dry this summer day would become, she'd catch a chill from the morning rain. "Whatever possessed you to go out in the rain?"

"Never mind, Bridget. It's nothing," she said as she slammed a paper-wrapped parcel onto the table and took the hot tea from my hand.

The cup shook as she drew it to her lips. I watched her curiously for a moment, waiting for an explanation, before my patience gave out and I lifted the package to my nose, breathing in the scent. Lately, she'd been unpredictable enough that I wouldn't put it past her to come home with something bizarre, like perfume or one of those scandalous books I'd heard Minnie talking about to Seamus. But this wasn't a book or even a new pair of stockings to replace the ones she had yet to darn. Whatever this was held an odor, sharp and raw. Lye.

"Washing soap?" I questioned, and Lizzie nodded.

"I was planning on washing Mrs. Borden's dresses this afternoon," I continued. "If you'd told me yours needed freshening, I would've done them as well."

"Mine are fine," Lizzie said, as she tossed a scrap of paper to the table and slumped down into the chair. "The lye was on your list."

I picked up the crumpled piece of paper, glancing at the handwriting. Every morning, Mrs. Borden left me a list of chores, the ones she wanted done first underlined three times. On the bottom would be the items she needed from downtown. A cheap cut of meat from the butcher, gray cotton for mending, lye so that I could do the wash . . . I had been surprised not to see the list on the counter waiting for me as I prepared breakfast this morning; I'd figured she hadn't finished it yet.

"This is the list your mother leaves for me each evening."

"Stepmother," Lizzie corrected. "And I thought I'd save you some time and take care of the errands myself. I couldn't sleep anyway, so I got up and took your list, thought I would help you today."

I shook my head and leaned back in my chair, quickly glancing down the hall towards the front parlor. If Mr. Borden knew Lizzie had gone to the market for me, he'd dock my wages. Wages I needed to secure mine and Liam's future. Money needed to buy Cara's passage to America.

"Your father—"

"Don't you worry about him," Lizzie cut me off. "He doesn't know, and even if he did, I'd make sure it was me he scolded, not you."

My stomach rolled with that thought. Lizzie was right. Mr. Borden wouldn't simply dock my wages; he'd find a way to penalize Lizzie as well, take what little solace she had and withhold it to teach her a lesson. I'd seen firsthand how cruel her father could be, how far he would go to make sure Lizzie stayed within the mold he set for her. And it wasn't good.

It wasn't more than six months ago that Lizzie had tried to take on a new charity, something to do with the temperance movement, combating the ill effects of whiskey, and her desire to minister to the morally inept.

I had laughed at first, thinking she could start in Liam's flat. I never actually offered that up, though. Knowing Lizzie and her outspoken nature, she'd take me up on the offer and march her pious friends down to Liam's dingy, cramped home, only to be horrified at what no doubt would be Seamus's crude response. Instead, I had wished her luck and hidden my small bottle of whiskey under my thin mattress, just in case she thought to save me.

She had talked incessantly about her righteous cause with Alice for weeks, until Mr. Borden caught wind of her plans. Apparently, he'd heard about a boy in that group, a young man no more than twenty-three who paid more attention to Lizzie than the others. The same one who had suggested her group start their mission with a visit to a pub on Corky Row. There was no way Mr. Borden was going to let either of his daughters be seen with a man at night, never mind outside a pub, and certainly not near Corky Row.

The two of them screamed until the wee hours of the morning, Lizzie countering her father's accusations with more than plenty of her own. But when all was said and done, when the screams faded to hushed whispers and eventually to sobs, Mr. Borden had won. Lizzie was left planning Sunday school lessons while the saving of Fall River's drunken souls became someone else's mission.

But that was the way it always worked in the Borden house. Any hint of life, any sign of happiness, was quickly quashed by Mr. Borden out of fear it was the devil's handiwork. Quiet, obedient, and utterly boring . . . that was the way Mr. Borden preferred his house. The way he preferred his women.

Chapter 6

"Bridget? Are you listening to me? I said I went to the market for you." Lizzie waved a hand in front of my face as she repeated herself.

"Please, don't cross your father again," I pleaded. I didn't want her to sink into one of her moods where cold silence permeated every corner of this house. "It's not worth it."

"Hush up about my father, Bridget. I said you had nothing to worry about when it came to him."

That wasn't true, and she knew it. Everyone had something to worry about when it came to Andrew Borden. If you owed him money, he'd find you. If you were a tenant with questionable associates, he'd evict you on the spot. And if you had no debt with him, he'd eventually make sure you did. Yes, Lizzie thought she could handle her father, but there was a look of dark intent in his eyes when he talked to her that made me think she was very, *very* wrong.

I stared down at the package Lizzie had brought back from the store, curious as to why she stopped there. Why, if she was so intent on helping me, had she only gone to the pharmacy and ignored everything else on my list? There were at least ten items written down, and yet she'd come home with only one.

"Why do you only have lye?" I asked, already guessing at the answer. Something must have gone wrong. I'd seen it happen before

. . . back home. I'd watched Cara go in to help Mama with supper, then forget what she was doing and use the dull edge of a spoon to try and peel a potato. Lizzie had that same lost look in her eyes, that same fear and confusion that, to this day, still plagued my dreams.

"Lizzie, what happened?"

She didn't answer, rather shook her head, her eyes darting between the list her stepmother had left for me and the package of lye still wrapped and sitting on the table.

"Tell me, please," I begged.

"Do they ever ask you about me?" Her eyes were soft, almost fearful, like a child's. "Do you ever hear them talking ill of me?"

I didn't know how to answer. The truth was yes, and not merely the shopkeepers and their employees but Liam and his friends as well. Everybody in Fall River had a bit of gossip to prattle on about whenever it came to the Bordens. They all knew them, or at least *of* them. They knew Andrew Borden had two unwed daughters—one who had been caught shoplifting items from the grocer in plain sight, the same one who openly challenged her father in public.

"They were talking about me, Bridget," Lizzie continued when I stayed silent. "The owner of the store and the two boys he hired to stock the shelves. They knew I was there. They didn't even have the decency to stop, simply lowered their voices and kept right on talking."

She paused for a moment, her eyes darkening as she lost herself in the memory. "I heard every horrid word that came out of their mouths. Do you know what they said? Do you have any idea what they actually think of me?"

I nodded. I'd heard it all before. She was a thief. The previous maid had quit because Lizzie took an unseemly interest in her. She was prone to fits of fugue. Once I'd even overheard the unthinkable—that Lizzie was taking up in bed with her own father and her stepmother knew, but simply looked the other way. It wasn't only Lizzie that they prattled on about, but the entire household: Mr. Borden, Emma, and Mrs. Borden alike. The gossip changed daily, but it never got better. Never stopped.

I looked at Lizzie, really looked at her for the first time in months. She'd lost weight these past few weeks, and the smile I rarely saw had completely disappeared. I hadn't heard her laugh or sing, and she was spending less and less time with her friend, Alice. Even the children at Sunday school no longer brought her joy. She'd complain about the lessons and the strict order she was expected to maintain. Tired and seeming wearier than her thirty-two years, Lizzie looked defeated.

As much as I tried not to, I couldn't help but wonder if this was my baby sister staring back at me some twenty years into the future. Cara was still a child—barely twelve—and didn't have the presence of mind to understand what most people said either way. But staring at Lizzie, at the woman everybody deemed odd and unpredictable, I feared this was the life Cara would have. The life I'd condemned her to.

"I wish you hadn't gone, Lizzie. Those people—"

She cut me off with a quick pound of her fist to the table. I startled back, frightened at how quickly she'd gone from hurt to angry. "Answer my question, Bridget. Are they always talking about us that way? About *me*? Do *you* talk about me that way?"

"Never." And that was the truth. Not in the letters I wrote home to Mum, not even to Liam or Minnie. I'd go on about how I had to tromp down three flights of stairs to use the cellar privy, and how Emma seemed to avoid this house at all costs, but not once had I ever said anything questionable about Lizzie. I couldn't. As much as it bothered me to admit it, I considered her a friend.

"I would never speak ill of you or Mr. Borden. Not of Mrs. Borden or Emma either." I paused for a moment, realizing that what she wanted . . . what she *needed*, was a strong dose of reassurance. "I would never speak poorly of you, Lizzie. I consider you a friend, like a sister."

Lizzie looked up, a calmness passing over her face. She seemed relieved, as if for a moment she had doubted me. "Thank you. I think the same of you, Bridget. You know that, right?"

Smiling, I patted her hand. "I do." As volatile as Lizzie could be sometimes, she was equally as loyal. She was telling the truth, something so many folks in Fall River seemed to find unnecessary.

"What happened to your dress?" I asked, eyeing the mess on her skirt from the knees down. It was times like this that Lizzie seemed different, almost vulnerable. Like all of her hardness and sturdy nature was nothing but a prideful act.

Lizzie shrugged. "I wasn't going to stand around and pretend as if I couldn't hear them. I told them what I thought of their sinful ways and left. I cut through the back alleys to get home quicker."

That was Lizzie, outspoken and not so mindful of her place. "What exactly did you say to them?"

"That their prattle was the work of the devil, and that I'd be damned right alongside them if I ever let you purchase items from their store again."

I sighed, curious as to which store I was banned from now. Errands that should take me no more than an hour now took the better part of the morning as I weaved my way past pharmacies, grocers, and fishmongers that Lizzie had had *words* with. "Which pharmacy, Lizzie?"

"Gallagher's, but I can tell you they won't be getting any more of our business again."

That pharmacy was a fair distance from here, but one I frequented often. I wished Lizzie would keep her outbursts contained to merchants I had no need of. If she could do that, then I'd be fine with her speaking her mind.

I set a fresh cup of tea in front of her and sat back down. "Want to tell me what they were saying?"

"Absolutely nothing," she said, waving me off. And to this day, I have no idea what those boys said to make Lizzie crumble.

Chapter 7

Lizzie was quieter than usual the rest of the day. She kept to herself, insisting on taking her noontime meal in her room. The only time I saw her leave the house was to feed her pigeons, and even then she looked somber. I didn't push her, knew better than to try to drag out the truth before she was ready. If she wanted to talk, she'd let me know. If not, then eventually she'd shove whatever was eating at her to the back of her mind and pretend it had never happened.

Part of me felt guilty for letting her wallow alone, but the other part was grateful because for once, I didn't have the weight of someone else pressing down on me. While she kept to herself, I didn't have to cater to her whims or spend countless hours listening to the stories she told about her father and stepmother, stories that would keep me questioning my decision to work here at all.

The sun was setting fast as I finished scrubbing the dishes from supper. I had intended to get to them earlier, but the pump in the sink room was stuck again and I was unable to draw water from the cellar. Instead, I had to trek back out to the barn, fill two buckets from the faucet there, and then haul them back into the house.

A creak on the cellar stairwell drew my attention. I looked up and found myself face to face with Abigail Borden. She'd been down there using the one indoor privy the house had. She didn't even meet my eyes as she made her way into the parlor, only the whisper of her skirts breaking the silence as she passed.

Mrs. Borden was a quiet woman, unnaturally so. So quiet that she preferred to write down my list of chores every evening instead of speaking with me directly. I'd asked Lizzie about her a few weeks after I started. I was concerned that perhaps I had done something to bring on her disfavor. Lizzie had laughed and told me the house was better off with her stepmother mute.

Mrs. Borden's heavy treads stopped abruptly, and I quietly stepped out of the sink room, curious as to what had caught her attention. My stomach dropped when I saw Mrs. Borden, and I took a step in her direction, pausing at the door connecting the kitchen to the sitting room. She was scanning the surfaces in the sitting room, first the tabletops and then the mantel. Either she was looking to see that I was attending to my dusting properly or she was looking for Mr. Borden's key. Both were plausible, yet something in the way she held herself told me it was the latter.

"Can I help you with something, Mrs. Borden?" I asked.

Her face grew more flustered as she paused in her searching. "Has Lizzie been in here today?"

Her question caught me by surprise. The sitting room was at the front of the house, directly behind the front stairs. It was nearly impossible to get from room to room without passing through it, and Lizzie passed through countless times each day to get to the kitchen, the cellar privy, even the barn. Of course she'd been in there. At one point in the day, we all had.

"Yes ma'am," I answered as I quickly glanced over the mantel for Mr. Borden's key. It was gone, but I wasn't surprised. He was home, up in the small office off his and Mrs. Borden's bedroom probably poring over documents at his desk. He likely had his key with him, would use it to lock himself and his wife inside that room when they retired to bed, as he always did.

She nodded once, her hand tracing the exact spot where Mr. Borden laid his key each morning as he left to attend to his business. I don't know why I did it, where the sudden urge to defend Lizzie from an accusation that hadn't even been voiced came from, but I walked into the room and cleared my throat to catch Mrs. Borden's attention.

"Lizzie's only been through here twice today, from my recollection, ma'am. Once to tend to the pigeons in the barn, and a short hour ago to take supper to her room." I purposely left out her early morning trip to the market, quite sure that would work neither in Lizzie's favor nor in mine. "I spoke with her both times."

"You speak with Lizzie often?" Her voice was low, and I had to strain to hear her. "What is it that the two of you could find in common to talk about?"

I couldn't help but notice the way her hands trembled as her fingers circled that same vacant spot on the mantel and the way her eyes darted around the room. She was nervous, and I would have given anything to know why.

It was in that moment, in the seconds I spent staring at her face, her hands, her posture, that she cracked. Simply slumped down onto the sofa and exhaled a giant breath.

"Mrs. Borden? Are you ill? Can I get you something?"

"Perhaps a glass of water, please."

In all the time I'd worked there, this was the first occasion I'd ever heard Abigail Borden utter the word *please*. I ran to the kitchen and drew a cupful of water from the fresh bucket I'd just brought in, then swiftly carried it back to her, quite sure she was about to faint. I'd never seen her so pale, so thoroughly distraught.

She was still sitting on the sofa, her eyes glazing over as she stared off into some unknown point in the distance. "Here you go, ma'am. Shall I fetch Dr. Bowen from across the street or perhaps Mr. Borden?"

She barely acknowledged me as she took the glass from my hands and brought it to her lips. "No." Pausing, Mrs. Borden did the strangest thing. She stared at the water for a moment, even went so far as to lift it to the last remaining light filtering in through the front window.

"It's clean, ma'am. I saw to that myself. The pump is stuck again so I had to fetch it from the barn, but it is clean."

Mrs. Borden looked at me as if seeing me for the first time. For once, she wasn't wrinkling her nose at the dirty water in my pail, or the stains on my apron, or the one unruly strand of hair that wanted to fall out of my bun no matter how many pins I used.

"How old are you, Bridget?" she finally asked.

"Pardon?" My mind raced with her question. It was one I'd been asked to answer several times since I'd arrived in America and generally, lying about it came easy. But not today. Today Mrs. Borden's piercing blue eyes were unsettling, the gentle tone in her voice unnerving me more with each passing moment.

"Twenty-four, ma'am." I silently cursed the small hitch in my voice as I spoke, desperately hoping she hadn't noticed.

"How old are you *really*?"

Mrs. Borden froze for a moment, and her eyes flicked back towards the doorway. I watched her fingers work worried circles into the arm of the sofa and had to stop myself from reaching out to steady them . . . to steady her. She caught my curious stare and stopped on her own, her leg beneath her heavy skirts taking up the same nervous twitch. She laughed, a small chuckle that was anything but pleasant, then took a deep breath as if trying to calm whatever thoughts had consumed her.

"You don't have to tell me, Bridget, but I'd wager you aren't a day older than seventeen."

I didn't answer. I doubted she expected me to, but she was right. I'd turned seventeen this past February.

When I'd first boarded the SS *Republic* in Queenstown, I lied to the men on the dock. I told them I was eighteen, then vowed never to look back as the ship cut through the waters like an iron giant. Age didn't matter much to them. So long as you had the three pounds to buy passage and you weren't showing any outward signs of illness, you were good. Nobody checked on this side either. They asked my name and age, then moved on to whatever poor soul was in line behind me.

Mr. Borden had asked my age, though. It was one of the dozen questions he had scribbled down on his paper. I told him I was twenty-three, a full seven years older than my true age. He wrote down my reply and moved on, more concerned with why I'd left the Remingtons' employment and whether I had a propensity for blathering about the goings-on of my employer's house then with my true age.

"It's no matter to me," Mrs. Borden continued. "You do your work without complaint and keep the gossip to yourself. But mind you, Lizzie is a fair amount older than you. Her past has not been without turmoil and her mind has suffered for it. She has sound reason to behave the way she does; both my daughters do."

I caught the last of her whispered words. She only referred to Emma and Lizzie as her daughters in private, when talking with Mr. Borden or their uncle, John Morse. Never once had I heard her claim them as her own to the neighbors or her sisters.

"I've done my best to protect them; I really have. But Lizzie is a grown woman now with a voice of her own, and she's refused my counsel. Her excitable nature prevents her from seeing me as anything other than a threat, someone who draws her father's favor and attention."

I thought about Lizzie, about how she screamed and stomped about in her room after fighting with her father. How trapped she must feel in this house, with the eyes of her parents . . . of this entire town always fixed on her. The very air in this place was suffocating, so thick at times that I could barely breathe let alone think straight. I couldn't imagine how it felt to Lizzie Borden, to have grown up with Andrew as a father. But if I had to put a word to it, it would be caged.

I thought of her father's voice, howling through the night as he chided her for being selfish or wanton. The way Mrs. Borden always steered clear, would escape to their bedroom and not reappear for days. And Emma . . . well, she was barely ever here.

Emma took it upon herself to leave Fall River as often as possible, frequently spending weeks at a time with friends in Fairhaven. It was obvious that her extended departures from the Borden house were troubling to Lizzie. Though she would never admit it, there was a cold edge to her voice when she spoke of her sister that told me the truth—Emma had the freedoms Lizzie so coveted.

I fought off a shiver despite the warm temperature. I didn't know what Mrs. Borden was trying to tell me, what her warning was supposed to mean.

"Miss Lizzie and I share nothing more than common pleasantries," I said, trying to assure Mrs. Borden and keep my job at the same time.

"I hope that is true," Mrs. Borden said as she laid her still full glass of water on the table and stood up. "I have no doubt that you are lonely. I can only imagine what it must be like to come to this strange place at such a young age without family or friends for support. But trust me, do not go looking to Lizzie for guidance or kinship. For your own peace of mind, for your own safety, *please* don't rely on Lizzie for that."

Chapter 8

I twisted my hair into a bun, pinning it tightly against my scalp so the dust cap would keep its hold. With a solid ten-hour day ahead of me and the midsummer sun beating down like fire, I'd take any opportunity to stay cool, even if it was something as simple as keeping the unruly bits of hair off my neck.

My quarters were nice enough, the angles of the attic ceiling gliding gently over my bed and creating a haven from the chaos of the house. But the heat was insufferable, worming its way into my drawers, the layers of my dress, and even my stockings. If it weren't for the cool rags Lizzie laid out in the kitchen now and then, I probably would've sweated myself into an early grave.

I slid my door open a crack and listened for the sounds of life downstairs. It was silent. Nothing, that is, but the sounds of the house settling around us and the knocking of a tree branch against my own window.

The massive clock down in the sitting room chimed seven, warning me to move faster. I smoothed out the wrinkles in the front of my skirts and made my way into the dim stairwell that linked my quarters to the rest of the house. The door to Mr. and Mrs. Borden's room was at the foot of the second floor landing. No doubt it was locked, but it didn't prevent me from pausing and wondering why he felt so unsafe in his own home.

The ancient wood creaked beneath the soles of my boots, and I slowed my gait, anxious to keep Mr. Borden from awakening if he wasn't up already. Odds were good he was already off at the bank or looking over one of his properties, but his exact schedule was of no importance to me. All I needed to know was whether or not he was in a favorable mood, and that depended almost entirely on Lizzie.

A few rays of sunlight streamed through the windows, piercing their way through the darkness. I ran a finger over the darkened wallpaper in the parlor, wondering when or if Mrs. Borden would allow it to be replaced. It must have been nice once, or at least fine enough for the servants' quarters in one of the houses on the Hill. But over time, it had faded, the deep blue background worn to a dull lifeless color, the white flowers taking on more of a muted gray tone, giving what was supposed to be the nicest room in the house a dim feel even on the brightest of days.

The walls in the kitchen were no better. They were painted a white that had been beaten down by years of stained mist. I walked over to the cookstove, intent on boiling down one of the aging lamb bones for stew. Mr. Borden didn't like to waste a single thing, insisting that the joint bone of under-refrigerated meat was perfectly fine to serve his family. I'd eaten better back home in Ireland. My father and brothers may have had no money to speak of, but what they lacked in coin they made up for with a respect for the welfare of their family . . . and with their hunting skills.

It was days like this when the house seemed to close in on me. The dull click of Mr. Borden dead-bolting the interior doors over and over again. The heavy footsteps of Mrs. Borden above me as she carried her chamber pot down the stairs and disposed of it behind the barn. Lizzie prattling on to herself as she recited her Sunday school lessons. It was these mundane and mind-numbing rituals that had me wishing I'd never given up my employment at the Remington house on the Hill.

The Remington house had running water and proper storage for their food. They had a staff of three, not only to split the day's chores but also to provide friendship and a bent ear at night when I was missing home and Cara. They were more gracious with their household allotments, setting aside generous amounts of money for fresh meat and sweets. And their carriage house was filled with useful items like spare wheels and lap blankets, not pigeons and musty trunks laden with rusty locks. But the Borden house was only two blocks from Corky Row and Liam. Plus, the pay was better, a whole ten cents more a week. Most likely that had more to do with the Bordens' inability to secure permanent help than with Mr. Borden's generosity. For the ten cents and Liam, I'd taken the position here.

I lit the stove and was reaching for the stew pot when I heard the key twist in the lock of the back door. Mr. Borden walked in, mumbling something under his breath as he kicked the door closed with his foot. Silently, without even acknowledging my presence, he dropped a bloody heap of feathers down on the table. I looked closer, gasping as I realized what I was seeing. Pigeons. Seven of them. All dead. All Lizzie's.

I walked over to inspect them, my heart stopping at the sight. Lizzie had raised those pigeons herself, coaxed them into the roosting box with the promise of a warm straw bed and seed. I'd watched as she handled them, as she spoke to them as if they were children and not wild birds. And now they lay there motionless, four of their heads hacked off, the rest bent at awkward angles.

Blood pooled around their bodies, seeping towards the edge of the table before dripping off and splattering in sickening drops at Mr. Borden's feet. I watched as he reached for a bowl and placed it underneath the steady stream of red—no doubt hoping to save it. Knowing him and his displeasure of waste, he'd probably instruct me to make blood pudding with it.

"Sir?"

I forced myself to make eye contact with him, nearly flinching at the icy cold of his irises. Andrew Borden and I had few exchanges, and even fewer conversations. What knowledge I had of him came from Lizzie, Emma, and unfortunately, the tattle down on Corky Row. None of it was good. None of it was sane.

"That should keep the prowlers away," he finally said.

His voice was gruff, gravelly; I didn't dare to argue. I'd heard him and Lizzie bickering last night. Mr. Borden had insisted the birds attracted indigent boys and thieves. Lizzie had argued that they were harmless animals, companions more than pets. They didn't come to an agreement, but I never once imagined he'd do this.

"Clean them up and spare nothing," he said coldly. "You can serve them tonight."

I swallowed hard as my eyes found their way back to the small, mangled bodies. He wanted me to cook them. Not only had he killed Lizzie's precious pets, but he intended to sit at the table, watch as I served them up, and wait for her to eat them.

"Perhaps I should invite Abigail's sisters to dinner," he added. "It's been a long time since they've paid us a visit, and I can't think of a more tempting offer than that of a fine meal."

Everybody . . . Mrs. Borden, even Lizzie's only friend Alice, knew what these pigeons meant to her. This wasn't about sharing a meal with family, rather making an example out of Lizzie. Had I not needed this job, had mine and Liam's future . . . had Cara's future not depended on staying in Mr. Borden's good graces, then I would have refused right then, given him a piece of my mind, collected my few belongings, and walked out.

But I didn't have that luxury. "Yes, sir."

Mr. Borden shuffled beside the table, smoothing a palm over the wrinkled suit coat he wore day in and day out. It was a mystery really, how a man of such means could manage to walk around in such ratty clothes and not care. My own dresses were as dull as dishwater, but at least I managed to keep them presentable.

"And clean that roost out," he added. "I don't expect to see any other creatures coming and going from my barn from here on out."

I nodded and immediately set to work on the pigeons, praying I could get them plucked and boiled before Lizzie saw them. She was already acting peculiar, and I was positive this unspeakable act would throw her into a tizzy. However filthy I thought the pigeons were, they gave her joy, and her father should have been the last person to destroy that for her.

Mr. Borden disappeared into the parlor, his footsteps becoming muffled on the rug. I picked up one of the birds and started the monotonous task of pulling out its feathers. It would've been faster to skin it, but that would mean losing the layer of fat under the skin, and Mr. Borden had already warned me not to waste anything.

I gagged, recoiling as the blood continued draining from the necks, seeping in between my fingers. The metallic smell hung heavy in the air, and I breathed deep, placing a hand around the still-warm bodies as I yanked out a handful of feathers. I didn't want to cook them. God knew I didn't want to even look at them, but other than Lizzie, no one crossed Mr. Borden. And I couldn't afford to lose my job.

I felt Lizzie's presence before I actually heard her, my trembling hands still tangled in the crimson feathers. I turned in time to see her storm through the back door, stopping short of the table. Her expression was pained as she reached out and gently fingered one of the few feathers untarnished with blood. With a single glance to her face, I saw it—the storm of anger that confirmed the very thing I feared. The eerie tension that had fallen upon the Borden household this past week was about to explode; and not me, not Alice, not even Emma returning to town, would be able to stop it.

Chapter 9

Mr. Borden was known for his foul temper and controlling ways. He was a miserly man. Some said he honored his money more than his family. But I couldn't complain; he'd been nothing but fair with me. He never spoke harshly to me, and up until now he'd never done anything sinister in my presence. But there were Lizzie's stories. And the rumors. Oh, the rumors. And today, staring at the agony swirling through Lizzie's eyes, I believed every single one of them.

Lizzie's jaw dropped, her steely gray eyes reflecting a combination of horror and disbelief as they skirted over the pigeons' bodies. The heat of the day made the smell of death stronger, and the blood was growing sticky in my palms.

"Do you plan to cook those?" Lizzie asked.

Her voice was unnaturally calm, as if the person speaking and the one staring wild-eyed at the pigeons were not one and the same. I nodded rather than answer. Besides, it wasn't my intentions I was minding, rather Mr. Borden's.

She stood there for a minute, her fingers gently stroking each and every precious bird as she mumbled something incoherent under her breath. If I hadn't known better, I'd have sworn it was the Lord's Prayer, followed by an oath to bring the hand of the devil himself upon her father.

I liked it better when Lizzie yelled, when she spoke harshly to her father, or told Mrs. Borden that Emma had been more of a mother than she ever was. What I didn't like, what made me nervous, was when she sat there like that, quietly stewing. That was when things got bad, when her fits of fugue would take hold, leaving her deranged and carrying on about a family curse.

"Lizzie?" I said as I slid the pigeons away from her hands. Letting her toy with them would only make things worse, more painful, when she was required to sit down with her aunts and make small talk over the evening meal. I needed to get them out of her sight. Disregarding Mr. Borden's strict instructions, I quickly skinned them and tossed them in a pot. I'd come back to season them later.

"Lizzie," I said again, hoping to draw her out of the disturbing silence that had settled around her. She looked up, her eyes piercing mine with a desolation I'd seen only once before—on the SS *Republic*. I'd nearly lost my life on the trip over to the States, had watched in horror as dozens of other less fortunate travelers fell ill with cholera. Their skin pallid, fingers curled hopelessly around their bedpans, until they finally let go. In that moment, Lizzie had the same broken look to her, the same, heart-wrenching desire to simply die.

"Have you ever seen the coop I built in the barn?" she asked.

I nodded. I'd been in the barn countless times, had been in there with her yesterday helping her stow away her fishing gear.

"Come." She got up from her seat and headed towards the back door. She held her hand out for the key to the spring lock, and it wasn't until I handed it to her that she continued on. "I want to show you the barn, Bridget. Introduce you to *all* the things it holds."

The tone of her voice was off, every word laced with calm disregard. Despite my reservations, I stripped off my apron and followed her out.

We had a barn back home, smaller than this and surrounded by the rocky hills that dotted the coast. I always laughed to myself whenever I heard Lizzie or Mrs. Borden refer to this place as a barn. With nothing surrounding it but city streets and neighboring houses, it seemed more like a musty old house than anything else. No animals, no bridles, nothing but some old trunks, a wagon that no longer functioned, and Lizzie's fishing gear.

She opened the door and the rancid, hot air that streamed out nauseated me. The barn reeked, pigeon droppings and musty trunks making it nearly impossible to breathe. But neither the smell nor the heat bothered Lizzie. She spent hours out here each day, claiming the space calmed her nerves and eased away the stress of the house. I could understand that. The footsteps late at night, the muttering in the walls, and the suffocating darkness of the house were enough to drive anyone insane. Especially someone as isolated as Lizzie.

The grass in the small backyard was higher than Mr. Borden liked, every mosquito in the whole of Massachusetts seeming to make its home in the overgrowth. I held my skirts up, barely managing to keep up with Lizzie as she charged towards the small sliding door that led to what I presumed used to be a stall.

Stepping over the threshold, I coughed, barely able to take in a solid breath. I squinted in the murky black, pulling back as I realized that the gore Mr. Borden had dumped on the kitchen table was nothing compared with the carnage strewn across the floor of the barn. I don't know how he expected it to get clean; he probably assumed Mrs. Borden would add it to her endless list of chores for me to complete today.

I reached for Lizzie's hand, but she swatted me away. "You don't want to be seeing this," I urged. "Please, come back inside."

"Nonsense," she said, not even hesitating as she walked right through the puddle of blood. "He wants me to see it, otherwise he would have brought them to the butcher or had one of his farm hands cage them and release them down by the river."

Frankly, I agreed with her. Removing the pigeons from the barn was one thing. Killing them and expecting Lizzie to eat them was wholly another.

A bloody hatchet lay by the coop, Mr. Borden's red fingerprints smudged across its handle. It didn't faze Lizzie, though; it didn't seem to do much other than spur her determination. "The only way to deal with my father is to know exactly *what* you're dealing with. Once you know that, then you can play his game. Maybe even beat him at it."

I took note of the change in Lizzie's tone, curious as to exactly what game she meant. But it wasn't her tone that had me stepping back so much as the fact that she had referred to her father not as a "who," but as a "what."

"You know my father was a carpenter," she continued as she backed out of the stall and started pulling tools from the hooks that lined the walls. "But did you know it was coffins that made him wealthy?"

I nodded. Liam had told me as much, even said Mr. Borden did unspeakable things to the dead to save on the cost of wood. My friends on Corky Row were always talking about Andrew Borden and his homely daughters. Most of the time I chose not to listen. But certain stories were impossible to ignore.

"Father was smart. He offered to give folks their money back if they were dissatisfied with their coffins." Lizzie chuckled and shook her head, though I failed to see the humor in someone's passing. "Funny, I don't gather many people have the ability to rise from the dead to complain, do you?"

I almost argued with her. Almost told her about the two tiny voices I heard echoing in the halls of this house at night. Perhaps they were here to complain, to demand to be heard.

I felt shaky thinking about it. I wanted nothing more than to get out of that barn, cook the pigeons, and be done with it. The sooner I got it over with, the quicker I could get on with my chores, finish my day, and escape the madness of this house and make the short walk down to the pub to see Liam.

"Your father has invited your aunts for dinner. I need to set the table and air out the rugs. I don't have time for this right now," I said, hoping she would let me leave without argument.

Lizzie shook her head quietly and said, "The rugs can wait." Her fingers grazed over the handle of the bloody hatchet before moving on to Mr. Borden's collection of handsaws. "And as for my stepmother's eager sisters, I have no intention of sharing a meal with them."

My eyes scanned the rest of the tools she'd assembled. There were dozens of them, from shovels, to axes, to hacksaws. I couldn't imagine what Mr. Borden used them for. I'd never once seen him do anything even remotely handy, but they'd been hanging in this barn for as long as I'd been employed here.

"Did you know this is my Uncle John's?" she asked as she held up a cleaver.

I nodded. I knew Mr. Morse had apprenticed as a butcher, still made use of his skills out on the Borden farm in Swansea. Why he had them stored here—in Mr. Borden's barn—was beyond me.

"Uncle John wouldn't have made such a mess. He would've killed them quick and proper."

I wasn't sure what *proper* was, but I didn't doubt Mr. Morse's skill; I had witnessed it firsthand when he brought back a salted lamb or pig from the Borden farm for me to cook.

"Now these are Daddy's tools from when he built coffins," she said, ignoring the question in my eyes as she yanked an old quilt off a trunk. I coughed at the cloud of dust she sent my way and backed up in search of clean air. I'd never opened these trunks.

I'd been warned by Mr. Borden himself that what lay within was personal and not for the simple, pilfering mind of an Irish maid.

Lizzie took a hacksaw to the lock. She broke it clean off in one swing, then pried open the lid, the old leather squeaking as it protested the intrusion. One by one she pulled out the cloth-wrapped tools and laid them out on the ground as if setting out silver to be polished. My eyes were drawn to the dull, serrated teeth of a bone saw, and I reached out, oddly curious as to how and when it had been used.

Lizzie's mouth twitched at the edges, and she picked it up, held it out to me like a present. "Go ahead, touch it."

I did; I ran my fingers across the rusted steel. It was unusually cold for having been tucked down in that dark trunk and stored away in a barn that was hotter than the devil's lair.

"You know what he uses them for, right?" she asked.

I shook my head, nearly positive I didn't want to know.

"More than once, he's created a coffin that didn't *quite* fit. You know, measured wrong so that the box was too short for the body to be laid to rest inside."

Lizzie picked up the saw and slowly ran it across the tips of her fingers. I watched as her skin pulled, indenting as bits of the blade dug into her pale skin. Never once did it slice through, not even a tiny nick or spot of blood. It was almost as if she handled them often, knew which spots were still razor sharp and how much pressure *not* to apply.

"'Waste not, want not,' Father always said."

I'd never heard him say that, but Abigail Borden said it to me plenty of times. Every night as I cleaned up after supper she would repeat it, reminding me to save whatever was left for tomorrow's midday meal. But I had no idea what eating two-day-old oysters had to do with coffins and bodies that were too long to fit.

"What are you saying, Lizzie?"

"I'm saying that he refused to throw away the coffins, wouldn't even consider using the wood for the fire. Rather, he made the dead fit, cut off their feet if he had to, in order to get them inside."

I paled at her words. So it was true.

"Have . . . have you actually seen him do that?" My voice trembled, my heart hammering away as I imagined it—Mr. Borden's sweaty, suit-clad body sawing away at the limbs of some poor, deceased soul.

"I didn't have to see him do it to know it's true," Lizzie huffed, swiping a stray tendril of sweaty hair from her forehead. "He's admitted to it, even bragged about it to Uncle John."

I recoiled, watching in horror as she pulled out the larger of the two saws. "See the teeth on this one? See how they're farther apart? This is the one he uses to get through the bone. The smaller one slides through the muscle easier."

"And this." She crossed the barn to a metal table that was shoved into the corner. She dragged it over to where I stood, mice droppings falling to the ground below. "This was the table he used to size them on. You know, figure out exactly how big the coffin should be, then make adjustments if necessary."

"Here?" I nearly gagged at that thought, wondering exactly how many dead souls had graced this house.

Lizzie laughed, somehow reading my thoughts. It was cold and empty, a bitter sound that left me feeling unsettled. "Not here, you silly child, and not in years."

I didn't take kindly to being called a silly child, or to being laughed at for that matter. "Why are you telling me this?"

Lizzie stopped, the tiny grin on her face disappearing, twisting into something akin to pity . . . or guilt. She reached out to touch me, and I flinched, angry and confused. "I wasn't trying to scare you, Bridget," she started, her voice soft and soothing, crooning almost like she did to her pigeons when she was trying to coax them into her hand to eat. "I want you to be safe. If you're going to survive in this house, you've got to know who you're truly living with. Nothing is sacred to my father, Bridget. *Nothing.*"

Shuddering, I inched back away from the saw, away from the horrible metal that had dug into the skin and bones of countless dead people. It was too much. The blood, the gleaming metal teeth of the saw, Mr. Borden's cold eyes, and Lizzie's peculiar behavior. I took three steps back, turned around to make sure she wasn't following me, then ran back to the house, back to the kitchen full of hacked-up pigeons and walls that seemed to vibrate with unspoken cruelty.

Chapter 10

I hung my work skirts on the back of the door, taking care to smooth out any wrinkles I could with the palm of my hand. Not that it really mattered; the sticky air of my room would do as good a job as any iron. I didn't have a lot of clothes—three dresses and two pairs of stockings, to be exact—but I put on the nicest of the three and headed out, hoping that Liam wouldn't see me for the poor, plain Irish girl I was.

The flat Liam shared with his five brothers was where everyone tended to meet. They all worked together at the Borden Mill; all but the youngest, that is. Seamus was employed at the iron works, making nails. Rumor had it he'd applied at the mill too late, missed getting one of the last jobs they were handing out, but I didn't buy it. I always assumed he wanted some space. If you ask me, Seamus purposely took a job where Liam wasn't always looking over his shoulder, reminding him to mind his place. I couldn't blame him, not when I knew how it felt to be under a watchful eye twenty-four hours a day. Still, even if Seamus didn't see it now, he would have been better off at the mill with his brothers. Fewer people seemed to get hurt there.

If I closed my eyes, I could almost imagine Liam there, his nimble fingers working with the fine thread that would eventually become sheeting. I'd never been in there myself, and he claimed I never would. Something about not wanting me to breathe the foul air. But I knew the truth. He didn't want me to see what he'd become. How the son of a landowner in County Cork was now spinning thread for pennies an hour.

I groaned at the pinch in my aging corset, wishing I'd get around to saving the money I needed to buy a new one. Lizzie had offered to get me one herself. When I refused, she'd tried to give me one of hers, even offered to help me alter it to fit my smaller frame. I couldn't bring myself to do it. I'd seen her corsets when I did the laundry. They were no better than mine.

The once white cloth of her undergarments was yellow, stained from the murky water of the wash. The bones of her corsets were so sharp they shouldn't touch the hide of a barnyard animal, let alone a woman of Miss Borden's station. She'd asked her father for a new one a few times, requests he never gave in to. First, he'd laugh, then he'd yell, and then he'd stop talking to her altogether. It was a cycle I'd witnessed so many times I had it memorized, yet Lizzie had never learned how to make it play out differently.

I sighed, recalling an incident no more than a month back when Lizzie and Mr. Borden's raised voices echoed off the walls.

"Who's going to be seeing your corset, Lizzie?" Mr. Borden yelled, a telltale sign that she was pushing him to his limits.

"No one," Lizzie snapped back. "Doesn't mean I don't deserve better than this, that I should have to suffer through the day only to go to bed with aches that never seem to dull."

"A new corset would cost at least one dol—"

He went to argue, no doubt to tell her how frivolous she was being, when she held up her hand for him to stop. "Money you well have."

I'd heard this argument a thousand times, the whole bit about Lizzie being denied luxuries the daughter of someone with her father's wealth should enjoy. It used to bother me at first; I'd thought she was ungrateful, but not anymore. Not after listening to John Morse and Mr. Borden go over the rental incomes of his properties. Not after serving them tea as they went on about the farm's profit or the interest the bank was paying on his savings. Mr. Borden could well afford a new corset for Lizzie; he simply didn't want to.

"You have seven corsets, Lizzie. That's five more than your mother had at your age, and dare I say, six more than you need." I watched Lizzie cringe at the mere mention of her mother, knew right then and there that any chance Mr. Borden had of backing her down peacefully was gone.

"Your precious Abigail has more corsets than she knows what to do with, but heaven forbid I have a new one."

That was a lie, and I knew it. I took care of Mrs. Borden's wash every Thursday afternoon. She had two corsets and they were in worse shape than Lizzie's.

Mr. Borden laughed, a deep, sarcastic sound that reverberated off the parlor walls. Apparently he knew Lizzie's words for the childish lie that they were. "Abigail is none of your concern. You need to focus on your charity work and preparing your Sunday school lessons. Worry more about making yourself useful around this house and stop dwelling on what you have or don't have."

An angry Lizzie I could tolerate. Even her yelling and carrying on like a spoiled child was easy to take. It was times like these, when she pushed all her emotions aside and spoke with a lethal calmness that made me nervous, made me fearful she was plotting something. Something that would have this house in disarray for weeks and me escaping to the dark attic until it passed.

I turned to leave, uncomfortable with the silence bleeding into the room and the tension in the air between her and Mr. Borden.

"That woman is not my mother," Lizzie said, and both Mr. Borden and I turned around, following Lizzie's line of sight to the back staircase. Lizzie knew Abigail Borden was standing there, had watched her stepmother pale at her words and then continued on anyway with absolutely no regard for her feelings. "Yet you treat her and her sisters with more affection than you do your own blood. You buy them houses to live in rent-free. But a corset for me, your very own daughter . . . that proves too expensive."

Lizzie stormed from the parlor, the front door slamming behind her as she left. No doubt she was going to find Alice, complain to her one friend about how miserly her father was. What she missed was the sheen in Mrs. Borden's eyes, the coins she had tucked in her hand, and the subtle way she tried to hide them in her dress pocket before Mr. Borden saw.

It wasn't until the following Tuesday that I finally learned what Lizzie had planned. Mr. Borden was summoned to the Knox & Charlton Five and Ten Cent Store. Lizzie had gone in for a corset, put the new one on under her dress, and tried to hide her old one amongst the racks. When questioned, she dared the sales clerk to remove her dress and check for himself . . . a task that no sane man within ten miles of here would even attempt. Mr. Borden paid for the corset, even gave the clerk a little something extra to keep his mouth shut, but the news had made its way through the Hill and mills alike before the end of the day.

Embarrassment aside, Lizzie had won. She'd gotten her new corset at her father's expense.

Chapter 11

The house was quiet as I slipped down the stairwell, every creak making me hold my breath for a moment before moving on. The last thing I wanted was to come across Mr. Borden on the way out. Especially after the pigeons. Something about the way his eyes lit on me lately made me anxious. They were dull, lifeless, like the very flame that ignited him when he was angry with Lizzie could also drain him down to nothing. Whatever demons he was fighting now, I didn't want them directed at me.

The entrance to Liam's flat was dim, the smoke-filled space so crowded I wasn't sure I'd be able to make my way up the stairs to the third floor without toppling into somebody. One of the Dillon boys—a red-headed lad no more than fifteen years old—was already staggering around out front, drunker than a skunk. That was no surprise; the whiskey was always flowing here.

"Bridget!" A squeal pierced through the noise, and I swiveled on my heel, grateful to see Minnie barreling through the crowd. True, she lived and worked next door to me, but lately it seemed as if our paths only crossed here at Liam's. I missed our talks; she was my one true link to my past.

Her cheeks were flushed and her hair fell to her shoulders in wild, untamed curls. I wasn't quite sure what she was doing, but from the rosy glow of her cheeks, I wagered she was having fun.

She pulled up next to me and locked her arm through mine. I gave her a squeeze, grateful to see a familiar face. She was the one person I'd managed to stay in contact with since we landed in New York. We'd been friends in Ireland, our bond only growing stronger when we were forced to bunk together with a dozen other unwed girls in the bowels of that ship. I'd learned quickly that an excess of time and a lack of space can either draw you close or drive you insane. For Minnie and me . . . well, it made us the best of friends.

"Have you seen Liam?" I asked.

Minnie shook her head. "No, but I've been outside with Seamus all night so I wouldn't know."

She dropped her gaze, fingering the edge of one of her dingy skirts as she waited for me to start in on her again. I studied her face, the hint of a smile still there. I knew that look, had seen it on her face multiple times in the last year. Minnie was pretty, beautiful even. Her long, slender frame and high cheekbones definitely didn't go unnoticed by the neighborhood boys, including Seamus.

I sucked in another breath of stifling air and bit my tongue to keep from saying something I'd regret. Minnie was a year younger than me, and Seamus was blathered. There wouldn't be a rational thought between the two of them tonight, more like an abundance of childish whims. I loved Minnie but didn't want to see her on the next ship back to Ireland. Without money, without a solid plan, she'd lose her station in the States and have to go back to her da. A da I wasn't sure would welcome another mouth to feed. Again.

"Liam has other brothers, Minnie. Other friends who aren't so . . ."

Every time I'd run into Seamus he was pretty much soaked. Doubt that boy made it a few hours without taking to the bottle, and I had no idea how long he could continue supporting himself, let alone Minnie should she find herself with child.

She laughed and shook her head. I could tell her every sordid detail I'd heard Liam rattle off about his youngest brother, but it wouldn't matter. Not me, not Liam, I doubt even Seamus himself could change her opinion of him.

A pair of strong arms were suddenly around me, yanking me from my thoughts and into the smoke-filled air. I whirled around, met Liam's bright blue eyes, and smiled.

"I didn't think you were coming." He tossed me a lazy grin, one I couldn't help but return. Even with ale on his breath and a day's worth of sweat coating his skin, he was hard to resist.

I shrugged. Originally, I'd had no intention of coming. I'd planned to spend the evening in the spare bedroom mending the seams of Mrs. Borden's dresses. But things were deathly calm in that house. Lizzie had refused to come down for dinner, had informed everyone—John Morse and Mrs. Borden's sisters alike—that she'd no longer be taking meals with the family.

I'd served the pigeons as Mr. Borden instructed, his wife's sisters complimenting the tenderness of the meat. The thought of it, watching them slice into Lizzie's pets, made me sick, and I'd left the room, claiming I was feeling ill. I'd snuck back down and finished the dishes once they'd retired to the parlor. There wasn't much in the way of leftovers, and I didn't bother saving any. I tossed it all into the back alley and hoped a stray dog or an orphan would devour the remaining pieces. At least then I'd be rid of them for good and could put the blood and the bones and the bits of flesh out of my mind.

Eventually, Lizzie would have to come downstairs, if only for the fact that she hadn't eaten before I left. I'd left her a plate—some bread and jam I had left over from breakfast—but I didn't want to be there when she finally emerged from her self-imposed exile. Selfishly, I didn't want to listen to her stories or have to lie and tell her it would all be okay.

"Lizzie and Mr. Borden were . . ."

"Having words?" Liam finished for me, and I nodded. "I warrant those two are always having words of some sort or another."

"Not always," I said, trying hard to remember the last time things seemed peaceful, when Lizzie wasn't talking about how her father's miserly ways reflected poorly on her station or challenging her father's authority. Sure, things had been quiet *today*, but in the Borden house, quiet and peaceful didn't always co-exist.

"You should find employment back on the Hill," Liam said as he handed me his mug of ale. I didn't much like the taste of it, but I took a sip anyway before handing it back. "I don't like you working for those people. Didn't approve when you first took the job and still don't now."

"But I took it for you," I reminded him. I supposed I could have found other employment with a wealthier family, one where gossip, and rumors, and "fits" weren't commonplace, but it wasn't a guarantee. Not here. Not when there were Irish families crawling off the boats by the day, each one of us vying for the same lowly jobs. Lately, it seemed like the only places not displaying *Irish need not apply* signs were the mills, and according to Liam, no girl of his would ever work there.

Besides, if I had taken work in a different house, I'd only see Liam every few weeks, and that wouldn't be worth it. Plus, Mr. Borden paid handsomely, more than the Remingtons, more than my best friend Minnie made working next door for Mrs. Kelley. He did it to keep me, or so I presumed. I was the fifth in a long string of servants Lizzie had scared away, according to the rumors. But I didn't frighten easy, and I needed the money.

And as for Lizzie, on her good days she reminded me a bit of my sister, the outspoken girl who never quite knew what to make of the world. On her bad days . . . well, I figured it was good practice for what was to come.

"Minnie said the Thompsons are looking for a new maid. Perhaps she could put in a good word for you."

I shook my head. "I need the extra money, Liam. I can't bring Cara here without it."

"I can ask about extra time at the mill, ask Seamus to pick up some extra shifts as well. We'll make it work, love. We'll find the money somehow."

"You're already covering Peter's shifts, and I doubt Seamus wants to spend what free time he has tending to my needs," I said, as I caught a glimpse of him and Minnie out of the corner of my eye. They were talking—laughing, more accurately. She was sitting upon his lap, one hand curled into his hair, the other around the glass he was holding up to her mouth. She looked happy, truly happy. Seamus did too, and I'd be damned if I was going to take what little time they had together away from them.

"Besides, there's more to it than money," I continued. In a way, Lizzie had become more of a friend to me than Minnie, confiding her darkest secrets to me, and in turn, I entrusted mine to her. I refused to leave her alone to suffer in that house, refused to abandon her to the whims and wiles of her father.

Liam went to argue, and I put my hand up for him to stop. "I don't want to talk about them tonight. I don't want to hear how Mr. Borden profited off the dead or bought his sisters-in-law a house so he could control his wife's family. I just want to sit here with you, forget about the Bordens and the mills, even forget about home for a while."

Liam saw the sheen of tears threatening my eyes and pulled me into his arms. "Then forget you will," he promised as he held his mug of ale to my lips. "Forget you will."

Chapter 12

It felt like a lifetime ago that I had said goodbye to my sister Cara and come to the realization that I didn't know when or if I would ever see my family again. But that didn't stop them from coming to me in my dreams at night. My father's worn face, the clamor of my brothers and sisters running amok in our tiny, cramped house, and Cara's constant and nonsensical chatter. I missed it all. I missed them.

I pulled myself upright in bed and sighed in relief as I realized that it was still dark outside. Good, that meant I still had time to think about last night, to relive every wonderful moment I'd spent with Liam, before I had to dress for my morning chores.

Liam had taken two steps onto Second Street last night when I stopped him, gently reminding him that being seen together at such a late hour would do neither of us any favors. He'd groaned and complained, but in the end, agreed. He knew full well Mr. Borden had no problem with my going out, but he'd made it clear he didn't want any of my drunken suitors around his wife and daughters. And to be honest, last night, that was exactly what Liam was. Drunk.

Lizzie was pacing her room when I got home, the subtle glow of the lantern beneath her door dying the second I turned the lock in the door. She'd been waiting for me to return home, no doubt still enraged by her father's cruel actions. I should've stopped and talked to her, at least asked whether she'd eaten. But I had a spot or two of whiskey myself, and I was looking forward to my bed.

Throwing my bedclothes off, I got dressed as quickly and quietly as possible. I smiled, my mind circling around the events of last night—dancing with Liam into the wee hours, his lean muscles wound around me and the not-so-gentle thrum of the music beating through my head. I'd been sweaty, laughing, and three sheets to the wind, but it was wonderful. *Perfect.*

I slipped down the stairs and into the kitchen, fully expecting to be alone in my morning duties. But Lizzie was there, seated on the stool by the window. I startled, drew in a sharp breath, and tried to slow my heart rate. Her lips turned up into a small smile, one I could barely see through the darkness blanketing the small space. I knew what she was doing, what that tiny, apathetic grin meant. She was up to something, and somehow, I was going to be involved.

"Have fun last night, Bridget?" Lizzie asked as she dropped another lump of sugar into her coffee, stirring it slowly as her smile widened.

I nodded, ready to take any ribbing she had for me. I deserved it. I'd slipped away to my own life, left her broken and alone to deal with her father's cruelty, rather than stay behind and comfort her. It was selfish of me, and I knew it.

"You were up late yourself, Miss Lizzie. Working on something for one of your charities?" I asked, foolishly hoping to change the subject and distract her into a more peaceful conversation.

"No. Just tinkering about with some books and things. Besides, I couldn't sleep."

I didn't doubt her answer. Lord knew, each time I closed my eyes last evening I'd seen those dead birds, their eyes morphing and changing until it was Lizzie's slate gray eyes staring back at me from their bloodied carcasses. It was the whiskey I had hidden under my mattress that finally allowed my mind to still long enough for my dreams to carry me back to Ireland. But now, sober and with the light of a new day to greet me, I could see them, could feel the birds' eyes watching me.

I finished tying on my apron and got my first look at Lizzie. Even in the dim light of the early morning, I could see the circles ringing her eyes. Seemed she slept less and less with each passing week.

"Were you waiting up for me?" I asked. Funny how the idea of Liam waiting up for me, worrying about my whereabouts and safety, was soothing, yet when Lizzie did the same, it set my nerves on edge.

"No."

I could tell she was lying. Lizzie could never meet my gaze when she was lying. Her father, her stepmother, even her uncle John, she could fib to with little difficulty. But not me.

Lizzie pulled a small envelope out of her dress pocket and set it on the table. "Emma asked that you post this for her."

"Has Emma left already?" I asked. I'd heard her come in yesterday evening. She was talking with Lizzie in her bedroom last night before I left for Liam's. The conversation had been brief at best. Not more than ten minutes after Emma arrived, I'd seen Lizzie leave the house and head out to the barn to do God knows what.

"No. The letter was here when I woke up," she replied. "I presume Emma is simply out, visiting with her friends here in Fall River. At least, her trunk is still here," she mumbled.

I picked up the letter and turned it over in my hand. It was addressed to the Brownells, friends of theirs in Fairhaven. I would've thought nothing unusual of it—Emma frequently exchanged letters with them—save this one had already been opened and resealed, no doubt by Lizzie.

She'd taken to reading everybody's mail lately, both incoming and outgoing, whenever she got the chance. She swore her family was plotting against her, trying to keep her trapped, unwed, and dependent on her father for the most basic of necessities. Most days, I tended to agree with her.

"What does it say?" I asked straight on. Lizzie had no secrets from me; she knew darned well I was aware she'd read it.

"Nothing much," Lizzie responded. "She's planning to visit them later this month, says she's hoping to stay on with them through the end of the summer."

Lizzie's voice shifted, a somber note worming its way in. She didn't like the fact that her own sister seemed to be avoiding her, avoiding this house and everyone in it. To be honest, I didn't like it either. Without Emma in the house, Lizzie had even fewer confidants, fewer allies, and she told me things I never wanted to know.

"Are you going, too?" I asked, knowing some time away from the stifling heat and out of her father's reach would do her good. When she shook her head, I let out a sigh of relief. Just because I thought she should go didn't mean I wanted her to. The thought of being here alone with Mr. Borden and his sullen wife already had me rethinking Liam's suggestion of finding new employment.

"I'd miss you if you left," I said softly.

She heard my whispered words and laid her hand on top of mine. "I wouldn't leave you here alone all summer. God knows what sort of asinine things Abigail would have you doing. Probably beating the rugs at her sister's house while they sit around, living off my father's good fortune. *My* good fortune."

This wasn't the first time Lizzie had mentioned her stepmother's sisters. The year before I got here, Mr. Borden had bought his wife's childhood home on Fourth Street, and let her sisters live there rent-free. Both Lizzie and Emma were good and mad about that for weeks, or so I've heard. Lizzie had carried on about moving out, and Emma . . . well, she told her father *what he did for them, he should rightfully do for his own family.* Lizzie said that's how she and Emma had gotten their childhood home on Ferry St. They had persuaded Mr. Borden to sell them the house they were born in, for a dollar.

Lizzie sat there silently watching me as I got the milk from the icebox. There was some bread left over from last night, but not enough for the substantial morning meals Mrs. Borden liked, so I'd have to think up something else.

Lizzie got up to leave, and I put out a hand to stop her. "I was about to start the morning meal. I'm going to get some flapjacks going, maybe fruit, and fresh cream," I said, hoping to coax Lizzie into staying. She'd been moody since the day I met her, but lately it had gotten worse. Longer bouts of silence. More hours spent in her room, door closed, and meals skipped.

"Please, it'll only take me a minute to fix more coffee, and I would appreciate the company."

Lizzie shook her head. "I eat in my room now, Bridget. I no longer care to share my meals with my father or Abigail."

Or me, I added to myself.

"I can help you," I practically shouted, praying she'd stop for a just a moment and act like the Lizzie she used to be, the one who was full of spirit. "The pigeons, I mean. Perhaps I can get you some new ones?" I blurted out.

It was stupid. Lord knows, it was probably the most ridiculous thing to cross my mind in a year, but I didn't care. Lizzie was closing in on herself, losing more and more of her life to the insanity of this house, and I couldn't stand to watch it any longer.

Lizzie stopped cold at my words and turned around, meeting my eyes with a sad smile. "Tonight?"

I nodded, unsure of exactly how or where I planned to find seven pigeons tame enough to wrangle into a sack. Not to mention, I was quite sure Mr. Borden wouldn't hear of having them housed in the barn.

"Excellent," she said, then reached into her pocket and laid a second envelope on the small table by the front door. "Make sure

Father gets this. It appears as though there's a problem with the farm manager in Swansea."

"Of course," I said, curious as to who else's mail she had stashed in the pockets of her skirts.

"You don't know how much this means to me, Bridget. To think that you would risk my father's wrath—your very job—to see me happy."

I nodded and tried for a smile, all the while trying *not* to think of everything I had to lose.

Chapter 13

It was ten past eight and Mrs. Borden had already retired for the evening. Mr. Borden was still in the front parlor, reading the day's news. I'd already washed the dinner dishes, set out the ingredients for the morning meal, and added more coal to the cookstove, making more noise than usual. Yet still Mr. Borden sat there, unfazed, as if he had all the time in the world.

He may have, but I didn't. I needed him to retire to his room, safely lock himself in and the rest of us out, so Lizzie and I could get on with our plan.

"Drop a pot," Lizzie whispered in my ear.

"I already tried that." Twice, actually, but no amount of noise made her father move.

"Interrupt him. Ask him if he needs anything before you go to bed."

"Done that, too," I replied. The answer I'd gotten was a dismissive wave of the hand.

It was odd for Mr. Borden to attend to the news and his mail at night, never mind in the front parlor. He had a small desk in the study off his bedroom that he reserved for such things. It was as if he was aware Lizzie and I were planning something, and he was subtly telling us he knew.

"Do you think he knows?" I whispered.

"Not a chance," Lizzie said. Then without warning she reached for the iron skillet and slammed it against the cookstove, letting it fall to the floor with an equally loud clatter. "That should disrupt him."

Mr. Borden barely muffled his disapproval as he rose from his seat and made his way into the kitchen. "I've managed to ignore the ruckus you have made this evening up until now, but this," he said as he stared down at the skillet on the floor. "Have you lost all your wits?"

I turned around, hoping Lizzie would have an explanation at the ready, but she was gone, leaving me to fumble around for a plausible excuse.

"I'm sorry, sir," I managed to say as I bent down and picked up the pan. "The handle was wet, and it slipped from my fingertips."

"Ten times?" Mr. Borden huffed out an exasperated sigh. "I am amazed you haven't awoken Mrs. Kelley next door, never mind Lizzie and Abigail, with all your clamoring about."

"I'm sorry, sir," I said again.

"Never mind your apologies. I have been disrupted enough by your clumsiness. I suggest you retire to your room for the evening, give both me and this house a little peace."

I nodded, then set the skillet gently on the cookstove. I made my way to the back staircase, my eyes glancing over the lock on the back door. Lizzie had purposely unlocked it, was afraid the catch of the spring lock would rouse her father when we left. I prayed he wouldn't notice, wouldn't descend into one of his paranoid states where he triple-checked every lock in this house on his way to bed. If he did, if he saw the lock had been tampered with, then it would be me and not Lizzie that he'd scold.

Mr. Borden was behind me, his steps shadowing mine and his breath lingering on the back of my neck, only adding to my already anxious state. I was grateful when he stepped off at the second landing, his shadow disappearing as he rounded the corner to the bedroom he shared with his wife. His door clicked shut, the sound of the massive deadbolt sliding into place thundering through the otherwise silent hall.

Slowly, I made my way up the remaining twelve steps to my attic room. My hand trembled as I reached for the doorknob. This was a bad idea—sneaking out, helping Lizzie trap new pigeons from the park . . . this was all a bloody dreadful idea.

I opened the door and nearly fainted from fright when I saw Lizzie sitting on my bed, her skirts bunched around her, as she sorted through the few pictures of home—of Cara—that I had brought with me.

Her eyes caught mine and she smiled, genuinely happy, before she held up a picture of my baby sister. "She looks like a sweet child."

"She is." I grabbed the picture from her hand and shoved it, along with the others, back under my pillow where I kept them. Lizzie knew about my sister, the accident, and that I'd taken the job here in her house for the extra money—money I planned to use to buy my sister's passage here. I'd even shown her these pictures, but somehow this felt different. Finding her alone in my room, sorting through the most personal aspects of my life, seemed wrong.

"What are you doing in my room, and what was the meaning of that downstairs? You nearly put me out of your father's good graces." Not to mention what her father would do if he discovered her in my room alone. At night.

"My father has no good graces," Lizzie said as she stood and smoothed out her skirts. "And what I did, Bridget, was get us out of here tonight."

She had a point. Still, it hardly made sense to test what little patience her father had by deliberately sneaking around under his nose. From what I knew of Andrew Borden, he wouldn't hesitate to dock my wages if he got frustrated enough. I needed this job, and I was quite certain that if Mr. Borden dismissed me from his services I'd never find employment again in Fall River. He'd make sure of it.

"Come on, get dressed." Lizzie grinned, grabbed my hand, and towed me towards my dressing screen. "The pigeons will be all roosted up for the night soon. I don't want to miss our chance."

I grumbled as I switched out my work boots for an older, even dingier pair. The lingering scent of oyster stew still clung to me, I was exhausted, and yet here I was, planning to spend my night tromping around the park to catch Lizzie a new batch of pigeon pets.

"Abigail is already sleeping," Lizzie said as she eyed the two dresses hanging in my wardrobe cabinet, fingering each as if trying to decide which one *she* thought I should wear.

"And how exactly do you know that?" I asked, worry needling me. For all we knew, Mrs. Borden was still wide awake, just as capable as Mr. Borden of walking out and catching us.

"I looked in on her. Stood beside her bed for a solid thirty seconds. Trust me, she's down for the night."

Though I was glad she'd done it, something about the image of Lizzie hovering over a sleeping Mrs. Borden was disturbing.

"I say we give my father another fifteen minutes to settle in, then we'll quietly make our way down the back stairs."

"Are you sure fifteen minutes is long enough?" I asked, continuing to second-guess my decision to help Lizzie.

"Positive. Besides, we don't have time to argue, nor do we want to risk waking my father with our chatter. Sometimes you just have to get things done, Bridget Sullivan."

I nodded, unable to miss the spark of excitement brightening her dark eyes. As much as I hated the idea of spending a night I could use to rest up—or see Liam—chasing street birds, it obviously made Lizzie happy. And that was one thing she hadn't been lately.

We took to the back stairwell quietly, and I held my breath as we passed Andrew Borden's door. Lizzie had slipped her boots off before she left my room, claimed that she'd be quieter, less apt to get caught, if she was barefoot. I'd kept mine on. It was horrible etiquette for any housemaid to act that casually in her place of employment, and I did not want to break yet another rule.

I breathed a sigh of relief as the kitchen finally came into view, then nearly rammed into Lizzie's back as she stopped dead in her tracks. She shoved the boots she was carrying into my stomach, practically pushing me back up the stairs behind her.

"Father. I thought you were going up to bed. Is everything all right?" Lizzie's voice was louder than usual and laced with a lethal sweetness.

"Everything is fine," he said. "But I would ask you the same thing, Lizzie. And why are you dressed to leave?"

I gripped the boots to my stomach and silently eased backwards up the stairs. Mr. Borden's footsteps were getting louder, closer. A few more paces and he'd be at the foot of the steps, and I'd be in clear sight.

"I couldn't sleep. I thought I'd head out to the barn and tie some new sinkers to my line." The lie flowed effortlessly off Lizzie's lips as she disappeared around the corner, likely hoping to draw her father's attention away from the stairwell. "The heat and all . . . well, you know how restless it makes me."

Recognizing my only chance to escape the situation unnoticed, I quickly climbed the remainder of the stairs, nearly tripping up the last two in my haste to hide. I shut the door to my room and let out the breath I'd been holding. I'd been crazy to think we could get away with this. Absolutely crazy.

Chapter 14

I despised the giant clock Mr. Borden insisted on keeping in the parlor. Apparently, it was a family heirloom that belonged to his mother. Mrs. Borden must have known the sentimental value it held for her husband, because she checked the time herself against her watch twice a day, had even spent a small fortune to have it repaired last spring. I found it odd that Mr. Borden was so protective of it, so obsessed with an item like that when he seemed so untouched by other family memories. I'd cleaned nearly every surface of this house at one time or other, polished the silver hidden in the bottom drawer, dusted the bookshelves, and was even charged with changing over the winter linens. But never in my cleaning duties did I come across anything that had belonged to his first wife . . . to Lizzie's mother, Sarah Morse. It was as if the woman had never existed. Every picture, her clothes, her wedding ring, even the certificate of death, were all buried away with her the day she died. The only remaining connections Lizzie had to her mother were her uncle, John Morse, and her sister Emma. And John Morse was as odd and unsettling as this house.

But that's not why I hated the clock. Part of it had to do with the thing being ancient, its intricate design requiring far more dusting than I had time to spend on any one piece of furniture. Or maybe it was because it chimed every hour on the hour, and the midnight chime always sounded louder, deeper than the others.

That was the witching hour, and I was almost always awake. It seemed that no matter how hard I tried to get to sleep or how exhausted I was, that ancient piece of wood would jar me awake, tolling like a funeral bell.

My bedclothes were stuck to me like glue, my entire body covered with a thin film of sweat that refused to go away. Lizzie had snuck a bit of ice in a bowl up to me shortly after our attempt at escaping the house, a treat I never would have taken myself given that the ice delivery wouldn't come again for three days. Mr. Borden would certainly notice the chunk missing. He'd have my head in the morning for taking it, was probably already in a foul mood from catching Lizzie roaming the house so late. But Lizzie would defend me, would say it was she who took it and not me. Unfortunately, that small luxury had melted hours ago, leaving me with nothing but damp sheets, sticky skin, and a bowl of lukewarm water.

I'd just started humming the drinking song Liam was so fond of when a loud creak pierced the silence. The moan of the wooden floor outside of my bedroom raised the hairs on the back of my neck, and I clenched the sheet tighter round my neck.

"Hello?" I whispered into the dark, praying that the sound outside my door was my imagination and not the beginning of one of Andrew Borden's paranoid fits where he'd fiddle with the locks while mumbling something about intruders and madmen. The locking, the pacing, the mumbling, the murmuring. I couldn't take it tonight; I simply didn't have it in me after all that had already gone on.

"Who's there?" I called out.

Silence answered me, and I shifted in bed, trying to tell myself it was nothing. I might have succeeded had the sounds not started up again. Tiny voices this time. They were crying, softly sobbing. I bolted upright, panic welling in my chest as the cries died out and drifted silently back into the walls.

I sat there in bed, staring into the darkness, straining to hear every sound. Nothing. The entire house, even the street outside, seemed cloaked in silence. Funny, but I would've given anything to hear Mr. Borden's angry voice chastising Lizzie for waking her stepmother as she roamed the house. I would have gladly welcomed the chiming of the old clock in the parlor or the bark of a dog as it chased after one of the rats roaming the streets. But the silence, the piercing sound of nothingness, had me up and out of bed, searching out another waking soul.

I threw open my bedroom door and took the back stairs two at a time, nearly tumbling down the last few. All the lanterns in the house were out. The kitchen, the sitting room, even the dining room were completely devoid of light. I crept along the wall, feeling my way through the house until I hit the front parlor. I pulled back the lace curtains, hoping the light of the moon would guide my footsteps, then scanned the shadows of the room for something, anything, that could have been making the noise I'd heard.

"Lizzie?" I whispered. She often roamed the house at night, sometimes conscious, mostly not. It happened more often when Emma was away . . . when her older sister wasn't there to block her path and guide her back to bed.

I held my breath and waited for Lizzie to answer, expecting her to mumble out a sleepy hello. I got nothing but that same old clock ticking away and the faint scent of jasmine drifting through the air.

Jasmine. That was Lizzie's favorite perfume.

"Lizzie?" I called out once more, no longer concerned that my raised voice would wake Mr. and Mrs. Borden. I'd gladly take the brunt of Mr. Borden's anger rather than wander around this house alone. "It's not funny. If that's you, tell me now!"

A soft but indisputable thump sounded from the kitchen. I gasped, resisting the urge to scream. The murmuring was clearer now, not nearly as sad and childlike as what I'd heard from my attic room, but disturbing nonetheless. With my back to the wall, I moved farther into the room, farther into the darkness. One of the shadows moved, its posture, its lack of grace giving her away. I knew from the hunched set of her shoulders and the inelegant gait who it was. Lizzie.

Her back was to me, but I could see the hazy outline of her full skirts and the shape of the bun she always wore. And she was talking. To no one.

I scanned the room as best I could, but didn't see anybody else. I don't know whether I was grateful for that or not. No intruder was good; Lizzie muttering to herself in the corner wasn't.

I stood paralyzed, unsure whether or not to race back up to my room and hide or make my presence known. If Emma were home, I'd wake her, then stand back and watch as she coaxed Lizzie up the stairs and into bed. But she'd left this afternoon without so much as a curt goodbye to her father or her stepmother.

Emma had once warned me not to wake Lizzie when she was in the midst of one of her fits. If I happened upon Lizzie in this state, she'd instructed me to leave her be and let Lizzie snap out of it on her own. But this wasn't like one of Lizzie's normal spells, where she'd quietly wander around the house with unseeing eyes. This time she was engaging someone . . . something, even if only in her mind.

"She's not well. She's not well. She's not well." The words spilled from Lizzie's lips like a chant, muffled and barely audible. She was moving around the kitchen in slow motion, pausing only briefly when she bumped into the back of a chair.

"Lizzie?" I asked, my voice shaking so hard I barely recognized it. "Who isn't well? Is someone ill?"

Lizzie didn't respond, didn't even act like she'd heard my question. She continued pacing the small space, her even tone, her monotonous chant, never ceasing. Her words began to slur, and if I didn't know better, I'd have thought she'd gotten into the small flask of whiskey I kept hidden beneath my mattress.

"She's not well. She's not well."

I stepped further into the kitchen and reached out to shake her. "Do you mean Mrs. Borden? Has something happened to your stepmother or your father?"

Lizzie whirled around, her eyes settling on me. There was a wildness there, a vicious abandon I'd never seen from her before. And it was all focused on me.

"Lizzie!" I screamed her name and shook her, hard. The last thing I wanted was to be drawn into her madness, or for whatever evil was trapped in her mind to be unleashed on me. "Lizzie, wake up. Now!"

She shuddered once, her eyes brightening with recognition. "Bridget? What are you doing down here?"

"Looking for you. Who were you talking to? Who is ill?"

Lizzie shook her head, confusion marring her face. "No one has fallen ill. Why do you ask?"

Slowly, her eyes searched the room as if trying to figure out where she was . . . who she was, and what she was doing down here in the kitchen in the dead of night. The stool in the corner was overturned, the sugared apples I'd left in a bowl on top spread across the floor. She reached for them, her hands trembling as she put them back into the bowl and set it on the counter.

"Did you not take care of the dishes this evening?" she asked, and I followed her line of sight to four knives laid out on the counter. They were perfectly spaced, aligned from smallest to biggest, as if whoever took them out was measuring their length.

I picked them all up and carefully placed them back in the drawer, refusing to contemplate for one second why they had been pulled out, or rather, who had done so. The mere thought of it had me shivering in fear, a fear that would do nothing more than stir an already agitated Lizzie. "Come on. Let's see you back to your bed," I said and reached for her hand.

Lizzie's hand was cold, her fingers almost white. Blue veins shone brightly against her nearly transparent skin, snaking across the top of her icy palm before disappearing behind the cuff of her sleeve. I put a hand to my forehead, grimacing as I brought back a palm full of sweat. The temperature in the kitchen itself had to be more than eighty-five degrees; my own body was still covered in a sheen of sweat from the humid night air. But she was shivering and huddled into herself.

Lizzie followed me to her own room, never speaking, never asking for or offering up any explanation. I turned my back as she stepped behind the partition and changed into her nightclothes. She reached behind her bed and tested the connecting door between hers and Mr. Borden's room, physically relaxing when the lock held the handle in place.

I settled her into bed and grabbed an extra blanket from the bottom drawer of the chest. It was beyond sweltering up here, but she was still shaking, the chills that held her body captive rattling her teeth. If she wasn't better in the morning, then I'd insist on fetching Dr. Bowen, find a way to pay for it myself if Mr. Borden refused.

"Here's some water. Drink it. You'll feel better in the morning."

She pulled herself upright and waited for me to settle the blankets up around her shoulders before meeting my eyes. "You heard them too, didn't you?"

I nodded. I'd heard them, but I had a sickening suspicion that Lizzie heard them louder, clearer, and more frequently than the rest of us. That the voices that birthed my nightmares were her constant companions.

Chapter 15

I sat on the edge of Lizzie's bed, my eyes trained on the flickering of her lantern. The flame was weak, likely the product of Mr. Borden's miserly ways with oil. Soon, we'd be sitting in a dark room. A darkness that, right now, I didn't welcome.

I hadn't gone back to bed. The silence of the house kept me awake. I'd come back in here a few hours ago to check on Lizzie. I stayed because I hoped the presence of another living soul would ease my fears.

"Lizzie, talk to me," I begged. She was sitting by the window staring out into the nearly vacant street. The pale gray of her irises looked silvery in the lantern light as she turned to face me. She looked lost, defeated, and utterly dismayed. It broke my heart to see her that way, to see the outspoken, odd, and uniquely feisty Lizzie Borden I'd come to know completely lost within herself.

"Maybe I can help," I said, knowing full well I had nothing more to offer than a bent ear. "Please, tell me what has you so troubled."

"Go back to your own room, Bridget."

"No. Tell me what happened down there. Please."

"You wouldn't believe me, and even if I thought you would, I can't tell you anyway." She paused and traced the pane of the window with a shaking finger. "I don't want you to be involved."

Frustration bore through me. I was already involved. I'd gotten sucked in the first week of my employment, when I found Lizzie wandering around the barn at two in the morning wearing nothing but her dressing gown. Back home, Cara used to wander in just the same way. I used to tell people the night air helped with her breathing. I used the same excuse with Mrs. Borden when she caught me and Lizzie coming back in.

I'd continued to defend Lizzie from that day forward, omitting certain information from Mr. Borden, and sometimes even downright lying about her whereabouts. Just last week, I'd found Mr. Borden's pocket watch hidden in the cellar behind the ash bin, the same watch he'd accused me of pilfering. I gathered Lizzie had taken it from her father's room, but I'd yet to say anything to either of them about it. I had tucked the memory in the back of my mind and left the watch where it was, hoping I could forget about it.

"No. I'm not going anywhere until you tell me what is going on." Being in this house every day, waiting to lose my mind, was bad enough, but for Lizzie to even suggest I wouldn't believe her, that I wasn't on her side, was simply intolerable. "Why were you fully dressed at two in the morning? And what did you mean by *'she's not well'*?"

"I'm not messing about, Bridget. Leave me be."

I straightened up and shook my head, irritated that she was shutting me out. "Have I yet to tell any of your secrets, Lizzie? Even one? What about the time I said I slipped, tearing your only good pair of stockings from the line as I fell, because you wanted a new pair and your father refused to give you the money, said he wouldn't replace them until they were beyond repair? He took the cost for the new pair out of my pay! Or what about when the barn was broken into and your father blamed you. *Again.* Who took the blame for that, who claimed to have accidentally left the barn door unlocked? Never once have I told them that you read their mail. You owe me, Lizzie Borden!"

Lizzie cocked her head as if confused, then shook it off. "I know what you've done for me. You've been more of a friend than Alice. But the secrets this house hangs on to are terrible, Bridget. Worse than you can ever imagine."

"I can't imagine anything much worse than you not trusting me, and that's exactly what you're doing."

I got up to return to my room, embarrassed by the tears stinging my eyes. It was true. Lizzie and I were close, had been for a long time, but something had changed in these past few days. Lizzie had changed.

"I'll see to your chores this morning," I said as I quietly turned the knob on the door. "And I'll make sure to bring your breakfast up so you don't have to see any of us."

"Wait. I'm sorry. Come back and sit for a minute, will you?" Lizzie's voice was soft, the words coming out on a sigh as if she was hoping to coax me back with a bit of information. "You know my father's Uncle Lawdwick used to own the house next door."

I nodded. Mr. Borden had mentioned his uncle once at breakfast. It was one of those rare occasions when he actually spoke to me. Lawdwick was long dead, but apparently he had once owned the land next door, residing in the low cottage next door until the day he died. But what any of that had to do with Lizzie shutting me out was beyond me.

"Great-Uncle Laddy had four wives, you know, but it was his second one, Eliza, that I'm going to tell you about."

A chill crept into the room and scuttled up my back, and I wrapped my arms around me. I wasn't in favor of talking ill of the dead, was sure the soul of the departed would find a way to curse me.

Lizzie's tone was even as she spoke, as if she'd rehearsed the story a dozen times in her head. "I don't remember Eliza. She died before I was born, but Father said she was quiet and kept to herself most the time. I was named after her, or so Emma tells me."

I couldn't help but look out the window and wonder if Minnie knew how connected her employer's house was to the Borden's. To Lizzie.

"She bore him three children. Holder, Eliza Ann, and Maria."

"The same Maria—"

"Yes," Lizzie cut me off, obviously irritated that I'd interrupted her story. "You've met her; she's married to Samuel Hinckley, although he's never been right since the war. Quiet, portly, not too bright."

I'd heard her use the same words to describe her stepmother, even her sister Emma on occasion. "What about the other two . . . Holder and Eliza Ann?"

"Doesn't matter," she said, waving a dismissive hand. "It is their mother that you should be concerned about. According to Father, she was prone to fits of hysteria, but they always seemed to get better. She holed herself up in her room after Holder was born. She refused to come out for days, refused to eat. Father said it was a hot summer, not unlike this one. Perhaps it was the heat that caused her madness."

Lizzie paused as if considering the possibility, perhaps wondering if the heat was to blame for her own recent state of fugue. I couldn't help but wonder the same thing.

"Uncle Laddy was out checking on one of his mills," Lizzie said as she visibly shook that thought off and continued on. "Eliza came out of her room that day, dressed in her shift, her hair uncombed and hanging down to her waist. She dismissed her maid to her room and gathered the children, then brought them all downstairs to the cistern in the cellar. One by one she dropped them in, watched them drown. Maria got away and ran down the street screaming for help."

The lantern sputtered out, leaving us with nothing but the faint glow of the pre-dawn sky to light our faces. I sat there paralyzed, so horrified by what Lizzie was saying that I could barely think straight. Eliza. Two children. Murdered in the well. It was all jumbled up into a wretched mess in my mind, a story I knew I would never be able to forget.

Lizzie was moving about, no doubt looking for some oil or a second lantern. Within moments a fresh lantern flared to life, illuminating her pale face once more.

"What happened to her? What happened to Eliza?" I asked.

"Great-Uncle Laddy found her sprawled across their bed that same day. She had taken his straight razor to her throat."

I'd never seen a picture of Eliza, but that didn't stop the image from flashing through my mind. Her body splayed out across the bed. Her blood seeping into the white linen. Her eyes lifeless as they stared into the darkness. Not unlike the pigeons' eyes; not unlike Lizzie's eyes.

"Why did your father buy this house if he knew what happened next door?"

Lizzie stood there silently for a moment, apparently lost in thought. "He said he bought it to be closer to his holdings in town, to keep better track of his tenants, and be closer to the bank. But the house on Ferry Street, the Grey house, even this one . . . it's like he is collecting pieces of his own history, trying to contain the curse that follows this family."

"Curse," I repeated, stunned. "Is that what you think?"

Lizzie shook her head and adjusted the flame of the lantern slightly higher. "No, I don't think he cares about what happened next door. I think he's as mad as she was."

Terror gripped me. Although I'd never admitted it directly to Lizzie, I was beginning to think she was right. Mr. Borden was more than simply peculiar. He was sinister. Warped. Touched in the head, as they would say back home.

"The fits you have, Lizzie, do you remember anything about them? Do you remember being in the kitchen or saying any of those things?"

Lizzie's face turned grim, ashen, in the shadows. "I remember hearing the crying and the voices. I remember saying the words now, but I don't know who I was talking to or why."

"You were saying, *'she's not well.'* What does that mean, Lizzie? Is it you who's not well?"

"Not *'she's not well,'* Bridget. What I was saying was, *'she's in the well.'*"

Lizzie shook her head, and for the first time since I'd set foot in this house, I saw fear, real fear, in her eyes. "You don't think it's happening to me too, do you, Bridget? Do you think my family is cursed? The madness that claimed my Aunt Eliza . . . the madness my father claims took hold of my mother . . . do you think is taking root in me?"

I startled at her words. Not once had I ever heard claims of Lizzie's mother being mad. What little I knew about her, what little I'd managed to glean from John Morse or Emma indicated that she was kind and gentle. That she had succumbed to an illness that often befell women. "What do you mean, your mother was mad?"

"Emma had some of my mother's things stored away in her dresser. Nothing of value, just a monogrammed handkerchief, a picture, and tiny bottle of her perfume. I didn't know she had them. I mean, I'd seen pictures of my mother, but I never owned any myself. Uncle John has a few, and he was always willing to answer all my questions. My father . . . well, I'd always assumed he was telling the truth when he claimed there was nothing of hers *to* keep."

I thought back to the countless times I'd laid Emma's delicates in her dresser. Never once had I seen any of the items Lizzie was talking about. "Where are they now? The things Emma kept, what happened to them?"

"Emma was packing her belongings the day before we moved here to Second Street. She had them on her bed and was carefully wrapping each of them in her stockings. I was twelve and excited to hold anything that once belonged to my mother. Emma told me no, and I yelled for my father, foolishly thinking he'd make her show me."

My heart sank at her words. I gathered that since coming into this world thirty-two years ago, Lizzie had yet to "make" her father do anything.

"He burned them. When he saw that Emma had them, he took them and threw them in the fireplace, destroyed every memory Emma had of our mother that night. Emma begged him not to; she carried on for hours. Father told her she was tempting fate, cursing this family with the memory of a madness he'd ridded it of ten years prior."

I quickly sorted through the rumors in my head as I tried to figure out what curse he was talking about.

"My mother," Lizzie said, answering my unspoken question. "The curse of madness he was referring to was her. Father once told me he stayed by her day and night through the last days of her madness, reminding her of who she was and how much he loved her. And in the end, she died anyway, something to do with her insides being all twisted up. But I know the truth. Emma and John know the truth."

"What truth, Lizzie?"

She turned away from me and sighed, her entire body collapsing in on itself. "What happened to my mother that night no longer matters, Bridget. But I do wonder if my father is right, if my mother was mad and I am damned to the same fate."

I did my best to smile with confidence although that was most certainly the last thing I was feeling at the moment. Petrified would be more accurate. For all the times I'd woken to Cara's mumbled words, for all the times I'd sat with her as she talked herself back to sleep, never once had her words been dark or tinged with the madness Lizzie spoke of.

"You're not mad, Lizzie. A bit outspoken and more stubborn than any other woman I know, but you're certainly not mad."

I patted Lizzie's hand gently, nearly gasped when she grabbed onto it and held it tight. "Don't leave me, Bridget. Promise me, no matter what happens in this house, you won't leave me here alone."

"I swear it. I won't leave you." No sooner had those words parted my lips then I regretted them. But it was the truth. As much as I wanted to throw on my day clothes and go running to Liam straight away, I wouldn't. If Andrew Borden really was a madman, if this house was filled with the spirits of drowned children and bleeding mothers, if there was *any* way that Lizzie was being dragged into the darkness herself, then I wouldn't leave her.

Chapter 16

Four hours. Four measly hours of sleep wasn't nearly enough to get me through my chores for the day. Especially when my mind kept wanting to revisit the terrifying events of last night. Lizzie's muttering and trancelike stupor, her insistence that there was a curse on the Borden family. It was unfathomable and yet so utterly believable at the same time.

I doubted Lizzie slept at all. She poked her head into my room just after dawn and told me she had some errands to run for the Fruit and Flowers Mission. Had I not been so exhausted, I would have questioned her, asked exactly what kind of charitable errands she could possibly be charged with at that early hour.

But now it was nearly noon, and she'd yet to return. Probably for the best. Talking about last night would only make it worse, keep it fresh in my mind when all I really wanted to do was forget.

Bending down, I rolled up the area rug in the sitting room and lifted it. It was old, the edges fraying, and the colors in the middle trudged out from Mr. Borden's constant pacing. I could barely keep a grip on it as I made my way down the back stairs and towards the fence that separated the Borden house from the rest of the world.

Panting beneath the weight of the rug, I couldn't help but think of Lizzie. She'd helped me with the larger chores before, claiming it was unfair for me to suffer because her father was too miserly to hire a second maid. These rugs would've been nothing for the two of us to manage. Between her sturdiness and my wiry strength, we would've had them beaten and laid back down in two hours flat. Instead, I'd likely struggle with them the whole afternoon.

"Bridget!" Minnie hovered by the fence, her face flushed with heat. Judging by the large basket at her feet and the clips in her hand, she was hanging out the wash.

Smiling, I heaved the rug over the fence and swiped the sweat off my forehead. I couldn't help but notice her droopy eyes, the pale look to her skin that told me she'd been out with Seamus the night before. She looked as tired as me, maybe even more so.

I laughed, thinking what a strange match they were. Minnie's innocent expressions, fair skin, and slight build looked downright misplaced next to Seamus's boisterous presence. I think that's why she was drawn to him. Where I craved predictability, Minnie seemed to thrive on spontaneity. Seamus made Minnie's life bearable, made her laugh when the world of Fall River regulated us into a bone-weary mess.

"Everything all right?" she asked.

I smiled, realizing that she probably had been chattering along while I was lost in my head. "Of course. Why do you ask?"

Minnie looked at the yard behind me as if to ensure no one was sneaking up to listen. I followed her gaze, wondering why in the world she thought anyone would be interested in our simple conversations. "What is it?"

She paused, her eyes wide and conflicted as she answered. "I saw the lanterns turning on and off last night. I could have sworn I saw shadows moving around, too."

I did my best to hide my surprise . . . and my anger. Rumors about the Bordens were already plentiful, and Lizzie most certainly did not need Minnie making them worse. "I couldn't sleep. The heat up on the third floor can be dreadful this time of year, so I took to the kitchen in search of better air. No doubt it was me you saw wandering about."

Minnie nodded, but her lips remained pursed into that thin, tight line. She didn't believe my story. I wouldn't either I suppose, but then again, I knew the truth, had witnessed it in eerie detail.

"But there were two shadows. And before that . . . ," Minnie trailed off, and I gestured for her to keep talking. The one thing Lizzie had taught me was to listen to everything. *Better to know what people are saying about you than pretend everything is fine,* she would always say. Something about it giving you the upper hand. Besides, I knew Minnie better than anyone—even Seamus. If there was something to find out, I'd get it from her.

"Before that what, Minnie?" I asked, coaxing her along.

She fidgeted with the stained apron tied around her waist, her large green eyes darting this way and that. We were friends, good friends, and she didn't want to answer. That couldn't be good.

"How long have you known me?" I asked.

"Since primary school."

"Umm-hmm, and who introduced you to Seamus?"

"You," she said, a tiny smile playing at her lips.

"You can tell me anything, Minnie O'Rourke. *Anything.* I'll keep your confidence, you have my word."

"Well, it's just that there was this noise. A sound that woke me up. I swear, Bridget, it sounded like someone singing." Her voice lowered, and she leaned in closer. "A nursery rhyme."

The beater I'd been holding slipped from my hands and landed in the grass by my feet. The story about the Borden children who died in the well came back to me, and I did my best to contain it, shove it back into the dark recesses of my mind where I housed all of Lizzie's secrets.

Minnie shifted in her place, grabbed another handful of pins from the basket, and set about hanging up the bed linens to dry. I knew what she was doing, I'd done it more than once myself—avoiding the obvious, avoiding having to process through a logical explanation for something that was clearly insane.

"Anyway, I got up and thought I'd been dreaming, but when I came downstairs and saw the light in the Borden house, I got to wondering."

I sent up a quick prayer for forgiveness, then started to weave my lie. "Aye, it was my singing you heard. The air in that house is heavy. You know how Mrs. Borden is, afraid opening the windows will invite prowlers."

I stopped long enough to judge Minnie's expression. She nodded, buying my tale. "The air in the kitchen was no better than my rooms, so I went outside. I don't take too kindly to the dark, ya' know, so I started singing an old rhyme Mum used to sing to me back in Ireland. Soothes my nerves, 'tis all. Sorry I woke you."

Minnie shook her head, the smile on her face bright and genuine. I wished I could do that with Lizzie, go and tell some silly tale and have her believe it . . . believe she wasn't going crazy, and that the unimaginable wasn't possible.

"You didn't wake me. I was concerned and wanted to make sure you were well. The stuff that goes in that house and all . . . well, I simply wanted to make sure you were all right. Liam would have a fit if he knew something was wrong over there, and I stood by and did nothing."

I muttered a curse under my breath as I picked up the rug beater once more and took a heavy swing. A billow of dust spread across the fence, covering Minnie's face. She coughed, two month's worth of Borden dust seeping into her lungs. Having Minnie next door was good, pleasant. But at times like this, I wished her blocks away, none the wiser to anything going on in the Borden house and unable to relay anything to Liam.

"Don't be tattling like the rest of the neighborhood, Minnie. We were raised better than that. The Bordens are fine people."

The Bordens may have been fine people, but they were also *odd* people, and the entire town, including Minnie, knew that. No doubt I wouldn't always be able to explain away the peculiarities of that house, but for Lizzie's sake, I'd do my best. I wouldn't let my own friends make her life more unbearable than it already was.

"I'm not tattling, I swear! It's only that—" Minnie stopped abruptly, her green eyes skirting upward towards Lizzie's room. The windows were dark, shut up tight with the lace curtains drawn across them. Nobody could see in or out of that house, and that's the way Mr. Borden liked it.

I followed her line of vision, only refocusing on her as I remembered my lengthy list of chores. Minnie's face was grim, her gaze dancing along the angles of the house.

"Do you want to hear what Mr. Alfred told me this morning?" she asked, and I swung my head towards the barn.

Mr. Alfred was one of the farm hands out on the Borden's farm in Swansea. I'd heard Mr. Morse and Mr. Borden talk about him often, bickering back and forth over whether he had the smarts about him to be the manager.

I hadn't heard Mr. Alfred come by this morning, but that was no surprise. He never came in the house, just repaired whatever Mr. Borden had sent for him to fix and moved on. I had no interaction with him, but the fact that Minnie did had me curious. No doubt it would interest Seamus, too.

I scanned the barn. I knew one of the hinges on the door was broken; Mr. Borden had complained about it the other day at supper. I presumed that's why Mr. Borden had sent for Mr. Alfred, but from what I could see, the hinge was still broken, the wood still leaning awkwardly to the right.

"When did you talk to him?" I asked.

"This morning, when he first came. He told me to mind myself in the heat." She flushed as she said it, the small smile at her lips telling me she was more interested in the attention she was getting from Mr. Alfred than in her employer's wash.

Mr. Borden would not be happy that his hired help was talking to the neighbors, would probably have Mr. Alfred's job for it if he ever found out. "What else did Mr. Alfred have to say?" I asked.

Minnie perked up and leaned over the fence, eager to talk. "Did you know Miss Lizzie kept pigeons in that barn?"

I shook my head and pretended as if that was news to me. I hadn't merely heard about it; I'd seen their bloody carcasses splayed out in the kitchen for me to cook. Their dead eyes, lifeless and fixed on me as if they were still seeing . . . still part of this earth.

"There are always birds roosting in the barn," I said as I took another swing at the rug. "They use the old hay in the loft for their nests."

"Not birds, Bridget. *Pets.* Miss Lizzie kept them as pets."

I tried to act surprised, desperately wanting to hear what gossip was flowing about Lizzie now. To most, she was an uncomely spinster who spoke her mind too freely. To me, she was the one person in this house that treated me as a person, someone to talk to, to share meals with.

"Now why would Miss Lizzie do something as foolish as keeping pigeons?" I asked.

"Don't know," Minnie said as she took another damp sheet out of her basket and snapped it into the breeze. "But Mr. Alfred says she would steal food from the house to feed them every day."

Lizzie hadn't stolen any food; I'd given it to her. A few crumbs of day-old bread or a handful of sesame seeds I'd stored for cooking.

"He told me a few days back, Mr. Borden got angry with Miss Lizzie about the birds, told her they served no purpose but to attract young boys and their cap guns."

"I don't recall seeing any boys hanging around the barn," I said. That was the same thing I'd told Mr. Borden when he'd asked about Lizzie's coming and goings last month. And it was the truth.

Not once had I seen a male suitor approach Lizzie. Not once, in all of our late-night conversations, had I ever heard her mention one. "Don't matter if they were. According to Mr. Alfred, Mr. Borden killed the pigeons anyway. He took an axe to their necks, then brought them in the house for Miss Lizzie to see. That's why Mr. Alfred was here, to clear the nesting boxes Miss Lizzie built in the barn and seal up any cracks."

I kept my gaze still, despite the clawing sensation in my chest. Funny how Mr. Borden was so determined to tear away every last piece of Lizzie's happiness, but couldn't be bothered with fixing the barn door.

"You sure Mr. Alfred isn't telling you some tale?"

"Aye. He showed me the axe himself. There was dried blood still coating the handle."

"Did Mr. Alfred tell you anything else?" I asked. If Mr. Alfred knew about the pigeons, I wondered what other tales he was spreading.

"No, just that it was nice seeing me."

The tiny smile that found its way back to her lips annoyed me, and I straightened my back to look her directly in the eye. I wasn't particularly close to Seamus, but he was Liam's brother and had gone out of his way to make me feel welcome in his family. Plus, he'd be *my* family soon, even have a room in the house Liam was planning on building for us. Because of that . . . because Liam mattered more to me than anyone else most days, I'd set my best friend straight.

"You should keep your prattle to yourself, Minnie. Folks around here don't hire maids who are prone to gossip. I doubt Seamus would much appreciate it either, seeing as Mr. Alfred is unattached and you seem more than willing to spend your time flirting."

I turned and walked away, afraid that if I stayed there much longer she'd see the truth I was trying to hide. The house I was working in was filled with crazy people, and everyone in Fall River knew it . . . including me.

"No, Bridget. Wait. *Please.*"

I stopped and turned around to face her. She looked scared, panicked. "Listen, Minnie," I said. "All I'm saying is that you'd do well to remember who Miss Lizzie is, who Mr. Borden is. Neither one would take too kindly to you speaking ill of them."

"You won't tell him, will you? I mean, Seamus . . . nothing is going on between me and Mr. Alfred. I swear it."

I let my arms fall limply to my sides, my muscles screaming from the overly aggressive beating I had given the rug. Minnie looked so small on the other side of the fence, so lost and confused, that for a moment I felt guilty. True, I lived in the same claustrophobic world she did, but at least I had Liam. I had someone to talk to, someone who listened and offered me an out, should I want to take it. Minnie had no one save Seamus. And he wasn't a day older than me, and not nearly as frugal or loyal as his brother. Best as he tried, I wasn't sure he could actually provide the kind of support Minnie needed.

No, I wouldn't tell him, not because Minnie was my friend or because I wanted to stop the gossip she was spreading. I wouldn't tell Seamus because at the end of the day, I felt sorry for Minnie. She was all alone in that house, her employer a widow who rarely ventured out of her room. A house that Lizzie believed was cursed, one that saw the death of two children and their mother all before Lawdwick Borden sold it. Despite all the yelling and hatred that seemed to fester in the Borden house, I wasn't ever alone, not really. I had Lizzie, and even on her worst days, it was better than having no one at all.

Chapter 17

Lizzie was sitting in the rocking chair I had tucked in a corner of my bedroom, watching me as I tied back my hair with a silver comb. She'd offered to help, even lent me the nearly empty bottle of jasmine water she had sitting on her bureau, all in the hopes that I'd give in to her demands and let her accompany me to Liam's.

"Take me with you." She'd been saying those same four words to me for the past half an hour, sounding more like a child of two than the grown woman she was.

"Have you gone mad?" I asked.

Lizzie scowled and went to get up from the chair. I held out a hand to stop her, only now realizing how cruel my actual words were. "I'm sorry. What I meant was, why in the world would you want to go with me?"

She brushed off the front of her skirt and stared out the window. She'd been staring off into space like that more lately, like the world was closing in around her and her only escape was somewhere off in the distance. Somewhere no one could see, not even her. But it wasn't the world suffocating her. It was her father. Unfortunately for Lizzie, there were only two acceptable ways to escape his hold—death or marriage—and neither one seemed likely anytime soon.

"I think it sounds like fun, Bridget. I mean, the only thing I've done this past month besides my charity work and teaching Sunday school is go to the market for you. I can't count on Emma, either. My days are starting to run together, and I feel like I'm slowly losing my mind."

"What about Alice?" I asked.

Lizzie laughed softly, that rare twinkle returning to her eyes. "You've met Alice, Bridget. She's as boring as a rock."

I had met Alice in passing, served her tea here a handful of times, but I doubted asking her if she wanted cream or sugar qualified as "meeting her." And as for the boring part, Lizzie was absolutely right. So far as I could see, the woman Lizzie shared her company with was meek mannered and impossibly dull. And that's the way Mr. Borden wanted Lizzie. Yes, Lizzie would have fun down at Liam's flat, probably more fun than she ever imagined, but that didn't mean I could ever cross that line and take her.

"Plus, I want to meet the boy you are so smitten with," Lizzie added.

"I don't think that is a good idea," I replied. Liam was already displeased about me working here, and I most definitely didn't need Lizzie's meddling to make it worse. She was getting more unpredictable with each passing day, her moods cycling by the minute, one second quiet and withdrawn, and the next prattling on about the injustices of society and this house. Not to mention, with the exception of the small bottle of whiskey hidden in my room, I'd never seen a drop of alcohol pass this door, not even an elixir to ease a cough. The Bordens very rarely cursed. They didn't drink; they never even danced. But at Liam's flat . . . we did all that and then some.

"I won't tell my father, if that's what you are worried about," Lizzie said.

"My friends aren't like yours, Lizzie. I wouldn't want you to think less of me." More accurately, I didn't want my escapades getting back to Mr. Borden. He'd have my job if I exposed Lizzie to what he often referred to as the "ill-mannered side of Fall River." Lizzie huffed and kicked back her heels. "My mind is not as closed off as my father's, Bridget. I thought you knew that about me."

"I do," I whispered. I had a year's worth of watching her purposely irritate her father to guide my thoughts. But I'd also been warned by Liam to keep my private life just that . . . private.

"Fine," Lizzie said, suddenly resigned to the fact that I wasn't going to change my mind. "But you can't keep him hidden forever. It's simply not fair."

She didn't make a peep for the few remaining moments I spent in my room. No advice on how to fix my hair, no complaints about my active social life that I purposely excluded her from. Only the creak of the rocking chair as she gently set it into motion.

I wondered if I should ask her to leave when I was done, if it was customary for the daughter of an employer to spend time alone in her maid's room. I decided against it. There was nothing in here worth hiding from Lizzie, and if sitting in the dark corner of my room in solitude brought her peace, then so be it.

"I can feel it getting worse, Bridget. All of it."

I had one foot out the door when Lizzie uttered those words, her eyes still focused on the nearly deserted street outside. Deep down I knew it was probably a ploy to get me to stay, to brush off Liam for the night and spend it with her. But *still*. Some tiny fraction of me wondered if she was telling the truth. If being here alone with nothing but the darkness of this house and the trappings of her mind made the voices she heard a little louder. A little clearer.

"Why don't you go see Alice? I'd be happy to walk you there. It's on my way." That was a lie; Alice's home was seven blocks in the opposite direction, seven blocks that snaked through darkened streets and decaying alleys. But if it kept Lizzie sane for one more day, for one more hour, then I would gladly do it.

"Don't be silly," Lizzie said as she stood from the chair, swiping her hands down her skirts as if the dust of my room had somehow settled there. "Alice would have nothing short of a fit if I showed up unannounced. Besides, I have some mending to tend to."

She left before I had a chance to respond, slipping down the back staircase to the kitchen. I heard the spring lock on the back door open, followed by the wood door slamming shut behind her. I didn't have to guess where she was going. I was sure she'd be in that barn most of the night doing God knows what. In the morning, I'd ask her, maybe slip into the barn myself and see what she had to toil over now that her pigeons were gone.

Chapter 18

Liam's flat was quiet when I got there; his brothers and his friends were all down the road at St. Patrick's. They all met there several nights a week, to give their thanks for what little they had and give back what they could. A few gave coin, most gave labor, but Father Fitzpatrick didn't seem to mind either way. The Irish had built that church, laid each stone, and now it was our turn to see to the repairs right alongside him.

Tonight, they were holding a prayer vigil for Liam's ailing friend, Peter Bence. He'd taken a turn for the worse this past Sunday. After Mass, we'd all head back to Liam's flat and drink to Peter's swift recovery.

I met Liam by the side entrance to St. Patrick's, was hoping to steal a few private moments with him before we joined our friends. I was expecting him, yet the minute I saw him standing there, smiling as if he didn't have a care in the world, I broke down.

The strength I'd harnessed all day, the calm, logical way in which I'd approached Minnie and Lizzie slipped away, and I sat down, right there on the side of the dusty road, without a care for the dampness seeping into my skirts. Tears I didn't know I was holding in fell, as the weight of the day and the enormity of the Bordens' secrets crashed over me.

"Bridget?" Liam stooped down in front of me, his blue eyes meeting mine. "What is it, love?"

I shook my head. I couldn't tell him any of it; Lizzie had all but sworn me to secrecy. That thought, the idea that I had to carry the weight of Lizzie's disintegrating world around, unaided, brought on another wave of tears. My body shook, each sob bringing forth another image. The pigeons, beheaded, with their life's blood seeping out into a bowl. The biting smell as I stirred in the barley and oats to make blood pudding. The tiny voices echoing through the walls of the house. And Lizzie, her story about the children in the well and her mother's untimely death. If she was right, if there was a madness consuming her . . . consuming *all* of them, I couldn't fight it alone.

"I can't do it," I whispered. "I simply can't do it anymore."

Liam sat down next to me on the road, wrapped his arm around me, and buried me into his shoulder. "Can't do what, love?"

I shook my head rather than answer, unsure I could find my voice.

"Nobody here is going to make you do anything you aren't willing," he continued. "My brothers and I'll make sure of that."

I grabbed onto his shirt and pulled myself further into his embrace. This was the one place I always felt valued . . . felt safe. All other reasons aside, that's really why I never brought Lizzie here. That's why I kept this part of my life hidden from her. It was the one pure thing I had, the only piece of my existence that wasn't tainted by that house. Only today, that knowledge hurt me even more. I was escaping, and she wasn't. Twice now this week, I'd left her alone with her fears so I could selfishly assuage my own.

"I can't tell you, Liam. I need to tell you, I want to tell you, but I can't."

"You trust me, Bridget?"

I nodded. I trusted Liam with my life, hoped one day to bind myself to him in the very church we were sitting across from. I'd never once lied to Liam, and often told him more than he needed or wanted to hear. Until now. Until Lizzie's unspoken plea to keep the fragility of her mind a secret.

"Then trust me with your secrets and let me carry that burden for you." His voice dipped at the end, as if it truly pained him to see me so weak, so utterly trapped.

He tipped my chin up when I didn't answer, silently begging me to see the sincerity in his eyes. "*We* are your family, here. Me and Seamus and Minnie. Let us help you."

"What did Minnie tell you?" The words came out sharper than I expected, and Liam rocked back, searching my eyes for a truth I would never reveal.

"Nothing." He paused and looked over his shoulder as if he thought Minnie or maybe even Lizzie would be standing there. "I haven't seen her in a few days. Seamus hasn't either. Is there something she's privy to that I'm not?"

I'd never seen Liam upset, never seen him be anything but gentle and kind with the people he loved. But I saw it then, that tiny spark, the indescribable potential for anger to consume him. "What. Does. Minnie. Know?"

"Nothing, not really. But she's been talking about the Bordens, asking about rumors she's heard."

Liam cocked his head, weighing the value of my words before he responded. "People are always talking about the Bordens. You know that; you've always known that. Why the tears over it now?"

He was right. Normally, the local prattle didn't bother me; I would shrug it off and go about my business. But the morning I'd seen Lizzie sitting in the kitchen, completely destroyed by what some stupid shopkeeper had said . . . well, everything shifted. The woman I saw as idiosyncratic, spoiled, and callous suddenly became real.

"Lizzie is my friend." I choked out the words, praying Liam would understand and let me be. Let me sit here unquestioned and cry until I felt better. "I can't stand to see them treat her that way. Not anymore."

Liam's hold tensed around me before he pushed me to arm's length. "Lizzie's not your friend, Bridget. She's the daughter of the man who employs you and nothing more."

That was the way it was supposed to be. The way it was at my previous places of employment. The way it was for Minnie. But Lizzie had a way of inserting herself into people's lives, drawing them into her own cracked world. Even Emma had cautioned me about getting too close, said it was one thing to be Lizzie's friend and quite another to live in the same house as her, to be her only escape.

"But you don't understand, Liam. She's lonely and Mr.—"

"The hell she is," he said, cutting me off. "She's neither lonely nor ill-treated, Bridget. What she is, is spoiled and manipulative, with hands as sticky as glue. Any problems she has with local prattle, she's brought upon herself."

I dropped my head into my hands, fully aware that there was some truth to Liam's words. If I wanted to keep my wits about me, if I wanted to outlast the countless other maids who'd cycled through that house, then I had do my best to keep my distance from Lizzie.

"She's not well, Liam. That whole house, that whole family isn't well."

I didn't need to clarify what I meant by "not well." Liam knew straightaway what I was implying and that this had nothing to do with a sour stomach or a bout of fever and everything to do with the smoldering, unnerving sense that something bad was about to happen. About to make things even worse.

"Has Mr. Borden—"

"No," I cut in. Mr. Borden had never shown an interest in me, never looked at me in that way even once since I'd started there. In fact, most days Mr. Borden seemed irritated and resentful that

I was even in his house. It was as if my mere presence were a concession he made to his wealth, that deep down, having a maid seemed too preposterous for his miserly ways.

"Then what? Lizzie?" he asked.

I thought about where to begin, what odd display of behavior I should tell him about first. The mere idea of putting words to my fears had me shivering, fighting off a chill that made no sense given the balmy night air.

"The pigeons," I said, hoping that if Liam saw the cruelty Lizzie was raised under, then perhaps he'd see her differently, understand why it hurt so much to see her broken and sad.

"What about the pigeons, Bridget?" Liam asked, coaxing me along. I'd gone silent again, trapped back in that moment, combing through each wretched second of that day. "Tell me what happened to the pigeons."

"He slaughtered them. Killed every last one of them, then wanted her to sit alongside Mrs. Borden's sisters at dinner and eat them." I swallowed hard. "He made me cook them. Told me I had to save the blood for a pudding. They were her pets, Liam. He killed them, then expected her to sit quietly by as I served them up for the evening meal. What kind of man does that . . . to his own daughter?"

Chapter 19

I'd never in my life seen Liam Higgins speechless, never seen his color so pale or his eyes so filled with fury. He knew full well those pigeons weren't there by accident, that they were Lizzie's pets, ones she'd coaxed in and kept well fed. I'd told him myself. Complained to him on more than one occasion about having to go out to the barn and fetch something for Mr. Borden only to find their caustic droppings had eaten through the leather trunk, covering its contents with smelly, white slime.

"When did this happen?" he finally asked, his words hushed as if he too couldn't fathom the depth of Mr. Borden's cruelty.

I bowed my head and focused on the grit beneath my boots. It was embarrassing. I'd made my way from Ireland on a boat filled with death. I'd found my own jobs and earned my own way, listened as Seamus replayed the gruesome accidents that had taken place at the iron works, and passed my fair share of child beggars on my way to the store. But I couldn't stomach the deaths of a few dirty street birds. With ten kids to take care of, my father would have slapped me silly for this kind of nonsense. Yet in the context of Lizzie, it all seemed so different. She *needed* those birds more than she needed a new corset or even a new charity to take on. They might have been filthy, but they were hers. The only thing in that entire godforsaken house that belonged solely to her. And now they were gone. Slaughtered. Dead.

"A few days ago. I know it sounds ridiculous. I know back home, we wouldn't think twice about stewing them up, but he didn't do it because they needed the food, Liam. He did it to hurt her."

"Why? Why would Mr. Borden do that?" Liam asked.

"I don't know!" I put my hands over my face, wishing for all the world I could just drown out this entire mess. Mr. Borden did it because he was a mean, vile man and probably as crazy as Lizzie.

This was my own doing. I had no one but myself to blame for not keeping my employment with the Remingtons, and for taking on a position in a house that was filled with so many secrets. But the houses on the Hill were too far away and my best friend Minnie worked right next door. I was only able to see Liam on my occasional day off, and I wanted to be closer to him. I'd moved because of him, and now I was stuck.

"She's having more fits, too," I said. "Muttering strange things about dead children in the well. She says that they are cursed, that eventually the madness will infect us all. I don—"

Liam held his fingers up to my lips, silencing me. "I've heard enough, Bridget. You know how I feel about you working there. I was willing to let it go so long as you were safe, but no more."

I shook my head. I was scared, and lonely, and worried about Lizzie, but quitting never once crossed my mind. "I can't quit, Liam."

"Can't or won't?" he asked.

I saw the spark of frustration as he did his best to keep control of his anger. Funny how he could break up a pub fight or bail Seamus out of whatever mess he'd gotten himself into without batting an eye, but Lizzie, crazy old Lizzie Borden bothered him.

I closed my eyes. I didn't want to see the disappointment in his face, the worry I was asking him to continue to carry, but I couldn't help it. It didn't matter that the house was slowly consuming me from the inside out. I couldn't go. I wouldn't leave Lizzie alone to fend for herself. I'd already done it to my sister, and I wouldn't do it again.

"Won't," I sighed.

"No friendship is worth this," Liam said as he leaned over and dried my tear-stained cheeks. I hadn't realized I was crying again, but the tears dripping down and soaking the front of my blouse were all the proof I needed. "Trust me, Bridget, this is for the best."

I nodded, some tiny piece of me realizing what he was saying made perfect sense. It was ridiculous to sacrifice my own sanity for anyone, especially someone who wasn't even family. Lizzie could help with chores and beat all the rugs in the world for me, but it wouldn't change the fact that she was Andrew Borden's daughter, and I was nothing more than a temporary resident in that house. One more maid in a long string of them.

"You can get another job on the Hill. I am certain Mr. Remington will put in a good word for you. Based on the gossip I've heard about your replacement, he'd probably beg to have you back there! And everybody knows how odd the Borden house is. Surely they wouldn't blame you for leaving." Liam took my hand in his, squeezing gently. "You can stay with me until you secure better employment. We'll lie, tell the landlord you're my cousin."

"With you?" I looked up at him, shock pulsing through me at the mere suggestion. On more than one occasion, I'd thought about what it would be like to live with Liam, to lie down beside him every night and bury myself in his arms. But of all the things I'd be willing to sacrifice to stay in the States, my reputation wasn't one of them. My da would curse me seven ways to hell if he knew I was even thinking about taking up with a boy without swearing my oath before God.

I shook my head, the reality of my situation closing in on me again. "I can't live with you. It wouldn't be proper."

Liam lifted my chin to face him. "Stayin' in that house isn't proper. You're safer with me, and you know it."

I thought about it, about what it would be like to wake up in a different house every day. One that was filled with laughter and smiles instead of darkness. Maybe one with proper refrigeration and electricity. A sensible privy, one that wasn't located in the darkest, most frightening part of the house. Most of all, no whispers. No hushed cries or creaking stairs. Maybe I'd sleep then, a full night of peace without the constant chiming of that clock waking me. Warning me.

"I'll talk to Minnie," I said, guilt for what I was considering already consuming me. "She heard the Thompsons were looking for a new maid. I'll go and talk to them, but I don't know if Lizzie will even let me go."

The moment the words escaped my lips, I knew it was the wrong thing to say. Liam's face turned stormy, every last bit of softness vanishing with my statement. "She has no hold over you, you can be assured of that. I'll come to that house and deal with her myself if that's what it takes. Her and her father."

"No!" I nearly screamed the word at him, overcome at the thought of Liam anywhere near Andrew Borden. I didn't trust my employer. I wouldn't put it past him to get so angry about me having a male caller that he'd do something irrational, make sure neither Liam nor I ever found employment in Fall River again. "You can never go there. You hear me? *Never.*"

"I will if that's what it takes to get you out of their grip." There was a hard determination behind his words. He meant it. Every word of it. If I didn't find a way out of the Borden house by myself, Liam would do it for me. "I can't do this, Bridget. I can't watch you suffer like this anymore. Not when I know I could stop it."

I flinched at the sheer pain darkening his eyes. "I'll do it," I said, "but I need a week to find proper employment." *And explain to Lizzie,* I silently added to myself.

Chapter 20

The clock at Liam's place read twelve forty-two when I finally pulled away from him and forced myself towards home. He'd held on as long as I let him, muttered the same set of promises over and over again in my ear. *He'd make this right, see to it that I was safe and far away from the Borden's hold.*

I slipped my house key from the string around my neck, unlocked the door, and took care to step as quietly as possible over the threshold. I didn't want to wake anyone and risk being subjected to a litany of questions about what I was doing out at this dreadful hour. All I wanted was to climb the narrow stairs to my room and fall into bed.

The kitchen was dim, barely light enough for me to find my way to the icebox for a glass of milk. But I could see Lizzie, sitting there at the kitchen table, waiting for me.

"Bridget." Her back rigid and her face blank. She didn't smile, didn't so much as twitch in the chair she was sitting in. Just stared.

I sucked in a breath and tried to remember the excuse Liam made me repeat back to him over and over before he let me leave. Something about a late-night Mass and a few special prayers for those in need. It wasn't a lie, exactly.

"You should be in bed, Lizzie."

"Couldn't sleep so I decided to get up and wait down here for you." She twisted her nightclothes around in her hands, the whites of her knuckles showing through the inky blackness. "I was worried, thought perhaps you met some trouble with that boy of yours."

"No trouble. We were down at St. Patrick's with some friends. The men were making some repairs to the church and the women—"

"In the dark?" Lizzie interrupted. "Must be hard to fix much of anything without the light of day."

I shrugged. There was no point telling her that most people, the church included, had electricity. That would only set her on a tirade about how backwards her father was, and I was too exhausted—mentally and physically—to listen.

"How long have you been sitting down here?" I asked as I poured myself a glass of milk. I held the glass bottle up to Lizzie, but she waved me off.

"A few hours. Maybe longer. Long enough to know that you stayed out with your boyfriend far longer than you should have. Your work will inevitably suffer tomorrow." She shifted in the hard wooden chair, her eyes settling on me. "Besides, what must the other employers think of our house girl wandering the streets at this hour?"

They will think no worse of me than they already do of you, I thought. "No one saw me if that's what you're worried about. I made my way through back alleys, and every lantern on Second Street was out anyway."

I shook my head and pulled out the chair beside her, intent on resolving this right then and there. Lizzie couldn't have cared less about what the others thought of me; she didn't even care what they thought of her. This wasn't about appearances, or reputations, or the quality of my work the next day. This was about me refusing to take her with me to meet Liam.

"I've decided to go to Fairhaven with Emma and spend the rest of the summer with the Brownells," she said.

I nodded. I wasn't exactly looking forward to spending any time alone in this house with Mr. and Mrs. Borden, but I wasn't going to try and stop her. Perhaps what she needed was some time away from this place, away from her father's heavy hand and the town's insidious gossip. Plus, it would make my finding new employment easier without her around begging me to stay.

"Is that what you want, Bridget? You want me to go there and stay with Emma? You want me to leave you alone in the house with them?"

"I don't want you to go, but if you need to, then I won't stand in your way."

I did my best not to sound too apologetic. Lizzie was already miserable, and I had no intention of adding to it. I'd certainly never imagined the time I spent with Liam would trouble her so, but I couldn't change it. I wouldn't lock myself into this dark home with her just to keep her happy and sane. I needed an escape, a sanctuary, a place where I felt safe, and for me, that was Liam. Perhaps the Brownells' house could be that place for her.

I heard a tiny scrape of metal across the wooden table and looked down, wondering what item Lizzie was toying with now. She saw me staring and pulled her hand back, the outline of a key remaining behind.

"Lizzie? Is that your father's room key?"

She nodded. "You'll want to keep this hidden while I'm gone."

I took the key and studied it, turning it over and over in my hand as I tested the weight. I knew Mr. Borden's key well, could tell you where the back was scratched from Mrs. Borden shoving it in the lock upside down. I'd moved it more than once off the mantel so I could dust, had even polished it once or twice at Mr. Borden's insistence. This key would fit the lock between Mr. Borden's and Lizzie's room, the door she had barred shut with her bed. But I was even more certain that this was *not* Mr. Borden's key.

"Where did you get this?" I asked as I slipped it into my dress pocket. Just yesterday, Mr. Borden had been carrying on about some missing papers, but he had his key on him and his door was locked. He'd had no one to turn his suspicions to. Not me. Not Lizzie.

"I had it made a few weeks back. Thought it be wise to have my own set of keys to every lock in this house." She put her fingers to her lips indicating I should keep quiet. "You don't need the rest, but this key . . . this key you'll need."

"Why would I need it? I'm not allowed in your father's room, you know that."

"He keeps a bit of money in the safe. The combination is 3-26-63. The date of my mother's death. There is enough in there for the trolley to Swansea. Uncle John is there, tending to some business for my father. If things seem odd here or you feel sick, I want you to take the money and go to Swansea straight away. Uncle John will send word to me, and I will meet you there, keep you safe."

I pulled back, astounded. I'd never stolen a thing in my life, and I certainly wasn't going to start now. And *keep me safe*? From whom? And John Morse would be the last person I would turn to for help. His mere presence caused me alarm.

Lizzie reached out and closed my hand around the key, leaving her fingers tightly on mine for good measure. "Keep it. I'll be leaving in a few days, and I need to know it's safe."

She stood as if to return to bed, but stopped short of the doorway. "Keep your wits about you while I'm gone, Bridget. You know how my father gets when I leave."

I did know. And my blood turned cold in my veins simply thinking about it.

Chapter 21

The rapping of the wind against my windowpane woke me up long before the sun normally would have. I brushed aside the curtains and peered out. Still dark. Still quiet. That meant everyone in the house was asleep, and I could get a head start on my chores. Lizzie was leaving soon, and if I had a prayer of finding new employment while she was away, I needed to start looking today.

I opened up the top drawer of my dresser in search of a clean apron and saw the key Lizzie had given me last night. I'd stashed it there, figuring it would be the safest place to keep it. I knew for a fact Mr. Borden would never go through my things, and Abigail Borden . . . she had enough with the temperature on the second floor, let alone the stifling heat in my cramped attic space.

I didn't want that key, wanted nothing to do with the door that separated Mr. Borden from the rest of us. But if Mr. Borden found out Lizzie had one made—or worse, if he realized I was in possession of it—things would go from bad to dreadful. I quickly tucked it underneath my extra pair of stockings and closed the drawer, hoping eventually I'd forget I even had it.

The steps to the cellar were dim, the light of my lantern bouncing off the walls and sending shadows skittering out every which way. Despite Mr. Borden's warnings against being wasteful with oil, I'd left another lit one at the top of the stairs. Should the cold air of the cellar extinguish my light, I wanted another to guide my way out.

I kept my eyes glued on the steps in front of me, counting each one in my head to keep my mind off the task at hand. I hated the cellar, always had. It was dark. Unnaturally so. In fact, even on the coldest winter nights, I'd make use of the outhouse rather than come down here to use the house's only indoor privy.

> *"Took a drop of the pure that keeps me heart from sinkin',*
> *That's the Paddy's cure whene'er he's on for drinkin'."*

I gave up on counting and instead quietly sang the words I remembered Liam and Seamus singing, focusing on the notes and the memories of them banging their hands on the table in time to the beat. I might not have had the best singing voice and I undoubtedly missed most of the notes, but it kept my mind off the darkness swallowing me and the whispers I could hear building in the walls again.

> *"To see the lassies smile, laughing all the while,*
> *At me curious style, 'twould set your heart a-bubblin'."*

The words rolled off my tongue as I reached into the stack of logs Mr. Borden kept for firewood. They were damp and I groaned, knowing exactly how difficult it would be to light the cookstove without dry wood. Blasted cellar. Nothing down there ever escaped the must and rainwater. Grabbing two logs, I tucked them into the folds of my skirt and quickly headed back towards the stairs.

I'd hit the second step when I saw a shadow cross the path of the lantern I'd left on the top stair. The lantern flickered once, twice, then vanished. Before I had a chance to call out, the door slammed shut, the force of it blowing out the lantern I'd brought down with me, leaving me alone in the dark, damp cellar.

I gasped and dropped the logs. "Mrs. Borden? Lizzie? Mr. Borden?" I yelled out, hoping someone was up and would hear me. All I got was silence. Eerie, empty silence. The entire cellar was veiled in a deep, vicious darkness, and it was difficult to see the steps beneath my feet. I stumbled up the next few steps, feeling my way along the treads with my hands. "Help, please, somebody let me out!"

I reached the top, panting, my breath caught in my web of fear. "Lizzie!" I screamed, rattling the doorknob. It was stuck. Or locked. I didn't know which, but either way, I couldn't get it open.

The door suddenly gave way, and I fell through, crashing in a tangled mess of arms and legs to the kitchen floor. I looked up, horrified to see not Lizzie but Mr. Borden staring down at me. His ice-blue eyes glanced from the cellar door to me, and back again.

"I assume you've got a good excuse for making enough of a ruckus to wake the whole household?" he asked.

I went to pull myself upright, and he extended a hand. "I'm sorry, sir. The door slammed shut on me while I was gathering the wood for the cookstove."

"It's not stuck," Lizzie's uncle, John Morse, said as he tested the knob. "Locked."

I hadn't seen him standing there, didn't even know he was planning to visit. Not to mention, Lizzie had instructed me to go to the farm in Swansea . . . to John Morse should things here become odd. How was I supposed to do that if he was here?

It was obvious he'd just arrived, which was probably why Mr. Borden was particularly sour with me. It was poor form to not have a morning meal ready for his brother-in-law, never mind a room prepared for him.

"I didn't know you were scheduled for a visit, Mr. Morse."

"Neither did I," Mr. Borden said so softly I gathered Mr. Morse didn't hear.

"I'll get your morning meal started, then see to your room." I looked back down the stairwell, horrified at the prospect of going back down there to fetch the logs I'd dropped in my haste. But compared with the alternative—standing in the kitchen indefinitely while Mr. Borden and Mr. Morse stared at me—I'd take the cellar.

I prepared to make my way back down when John Morse reached out and grabbed my shoulder. "I'll see to the wood," he said as he handed me the black leather bag in his hand. It was heavy, felt like it was packed full of rocks. Probably was. If I'd learned anything about this family in the past year, it was that rules of normalcy didn't apply.

I moved in the direction of the back stairwell, whatever was in that bag clinking like metal on metal. It reminded me of the day I'd arrived in New York, when I sat on the docks, listening to the metal cleats banging against the ship's masts in the fog as I watched them unload the dead from the bowels of our ship. It wasn't a good sound. It wasn't a good memory.

"I need those kept safe while I'm here," Mr. Morse called after me as I rounded the first set of stairs. "And they need to be stored in the barn."

The barn. The only place I hated more than the cellar was that rat-infested place.

I dropped the bag in the upstairs hall. I'd come back for it after I had Mr. Morse's room set up, and lug it back down the stairs.

The guest room was in the front of the house. It was the first room you saw at the top of the second-floor landing, one of the only rooms that wasn't connected to Lizzie's bedroom, which meant he could come and go unnoticed. John Morse did that frequently—left at ungodly hours to "run errands" for Mr. Borden, only to show up unannounced weeks later.

I opened the door to the room and noticed the bed was covered with dresses, the sewing cabinet open and the spools freshly wound.

"Bridget." I felt Mrs. Borden's pudgy hand on my shoulder and turned around, already knowing what she was going to say. "Please set up John in the room next to yours on the third floor."

"In the attic instead of the guest room? Won't it be a bit hot for Mr. Morse?" Truth was, I couldn't care less about his comfort. I simply didn't want him in the room next to mine, separated only by a flimsy wall and a door that didn't even lock.

John's deep laugh echoed off the walls. I hadn't realized he'd followed me up the stairs. "I'm quite certain that if you can stand the heat up there, I can as well, my dear."

I did my best to ignore the condescending tone in his voice, as well as the fact that he'd taken to calling me "dear" in his last couple visits. Glancing back towards Lizzie's room, I looked for any sign of her. At the very least, she would be able to keep him occupied. She'd prattle on about her father's willful neglect of the house when it came to things like indoor plumbing or an extra lantern for the parlor. She'd undoubtedly complain about his tight fist, bringing up how much money he spent on Mrs. Borden's sisters while refusing her the finer things. Mr. Morse would listen, nodding every few sentences, but I'd never heard him broach the subject with Mr. Borden. No, it was as if Mr. Morse was the keeper of secrets, a sounding board and a trusted confidant for the women of the house.

All the women but me, that is. I didn't like him, never mind trust him.

"Bridget," Mrs. Borden said, her hand waving towards the attic before she turned to Mr. Morse and smiled. "I'm sorry for the inconvenience, John, but we had no notice of your arrival, and the guest room is currently in use, as you can see."

"No matter, Abigail," he said, flashing a charming grin. "The attic room will do fine." Pausing, he met her gaze for a moment, the two of them exchanging a glance I would have given anything to be able to read. "I might be here a bit longer than usual. I hope my prolonged stay won't cause you any undue stress."

"Of course not. You're welcome here as long as you need," she responded, the wrinkles in her forehead smoothing out. I had no idea why she seemed so much calmer, or why yet another extended visit from John Morse would provide her relief.

"Andrew is having a few difficulties with some tenants, perhaps you could see to them while you're here," Abigail suggested.

"Of course," John said as he pushed past me towards the staircase, nodding in Mrs. Borden's direction. Something was amiss with those two. I'd wager she was the reason he was here. Mr. Borden frequently had problems with his tenants. If it wasn't him complaining about the quality of their business dealings, then it was them bellyaching about Mr. Borden's unannounced increase in the water tax or rent. But never once had he called John Morse in to handle his "difficulties." He took care of them on his own, honestly seemed to take pleasure in treating folks with disdain.

I quickly followed after Mr. Morse. The breakfast could wait. The sooner I got him settled into his room, the faster I could find Lizzie and figure out what was going on.

Chapter 22

Three hours. John Morse had only been in the house for a total of three hours, and I'd already lost my patience with him. Puttering about, opening random cupboards, testing locks, and muttering to himself. He was a nightmare. A living, breathing nightmare. Sometimes I swore he was nothing more than Lizzie in male form.

Lizzie herself was nowhere to be found. She'd left me a lengthy list of items that needed mending and articles to be purchased for the extended vacation she was planning. She didn't even have the decency to give me the list herself, rather left it in the kitchen next to the stew pot I'd taken down for dinner. Of course she had; she was still angry with me.

Half of me wanted to talk to her about last night and our discussion in the kitchen. She'd been angry, I'd been defensive, and the whole thing left me feeling sour. The other half wanted to wring her neck. Hired help or not, I was her friend and I deserved at least a little consideration for having quietly put up with her antics and covering up her missteps.

I lifted my skirt out of the dirt on the barn floor and stomped my feet loudly like Lizzie had taught me. I remembered the first time she'd showed me that trick. It was my first week of employment and Mrs. Borden had sent me to the barn to fetch the trunk in which she stored her winter garments. The mice were scampering about in broad daylight, and I could barely stand it.

Their beady eyes, their buck teeth, their matted and sickly-looking fur practically brushing over my new work boots. It was enough to send me right back to the Remingtons' house to beg for my job back.

But Lizzie wouldn't hear of it. She knew full well that if I left that barn without her stepmother's garments, I'd lose not only my job, but any future chance I had of earning a living in Fall River. So instead, she fetched the trunk herself, showed me how to stomp loudly and kick at the storage crates to keep unwanted rodents away.

I'd done it every single time I entered the barn since then, but the sight of them fleeing through the tiny holes in the wall still made me squirm. For somebody who was so concerned about the cleanliness of her rugs and windows, Abigail Borden sure didn't give much thought to where she stored her clothes.

I stopped just short of the fishing supplies and stared down in confusion at John Morse's black bag sitting on the ground. I'd completely forgotten about it, had left it on the second-floor landing. Mr. Morse must have moved it here himself.

I nudged the bag with my toe, and my initial instincts were correct. Whatever was inside it was heavy and irregularly shaped.

Peering back towards the barn door, I stared at the opening. Given the time, I was certain that Mr. Borden was at one of his properties and his wife was likely resting. But John . . . I had no notion of where he might be.

Slowly, I unzipped the bag, pushed aside the dark leather, and peered in. The sharp glint of metal caught my eye, and I opened the bag wide. One by one, I pulled out the items and laid them at my feet. I knew Mr. Morse had apprenticed under a butcher, knew he was living with that same man and his family now. The cleaver and the boning knives made sense, but the axe? Plus, I couldn't fathom why was he was carrying his trade tools around with him.

Yes, he claimed he might be here a bit longer than usual, but surely he wasn't planning on butchering anything in Fall River.

The tools were clean. The wooden handles looked marred from use, but the metal looked freshly oiled. And sharp. I would have paid a pretty penny to have these in the kitchen when I worked. They could slice through the mutton bones with little to no effort. But so far as I could tell, John didn't cook. He never so much as boiled his own water for tea.

I placed the tools back in the bag, careful to make sure each went back in the exact same position. I'd ask Lizzie later, pretend I had no inkling as to what was in the bag. Hopefully, she'd tell me the truth about why her uncle would be carrying such items around, but I doubted it. As kind as Lizzie could be, she could also be secretive.

"Oh good, you found my bag," Mr. Morse said. He was nothing more than a shadow in the doorway, his tall form blocking out the noonday sun. "I wondered where you put it."

I shook my head. "I left it in the hall, sir. Perhaps Lizzie moved it here."

"Doubtful. Lizzie's been gone for hours now. She left this morning for the Brownells'."

This morning? Wait, this morning? It was only last evening she told me she was leaving. When did she pack and what was with the list of errands she'd left for me to do? "I think you're mistaken, sir. Lizzie isn't scheduled to leave for a couple days yet. She gave me a list of mending she needed done just this morning."

I pulled the handwritten list from my apron pocket and held it up, as if that would make what he was saying untrue. Mr. Morse saw my confusion and his eyes softened.

"I saw her off on the train myself, Bridget. I thought . . . being that you and Lizzie seem to be so close, that she would've at least sought you out to say goodbye."

I shook my head, my mind shifting between emotions. Panic, confusion, anger, betrayal. I wished my body would settle on one, give me some raw energy to embrace. "She said she was leaving. She just didn't say anything about leaving today."

I turned and ran from the barn, not caring that Mr. Morse was calling after me. I tripped on the stone step of the back door, would have fallen straight through the screen had Mr. Morse not hooked his hand around my waist and pulled me backwards.

"Did something I say startle you, Bridget?"

Mr. Morse met my eyes with a piercing gaze, and I pulled back. *Not something, someone. You.* Usually I prided myself on my instincts, could sort out the good from the bad fairly easily. But not with John Morse. He was an anomaly, someone who had shown me nothing but kindness and respect, but yet I still couldn't bring myself to trust.

Chapter 23

"She's gone. She just got up and left without so much as a goodbye."

I'd been repeating the same set of words to Liam for the last half-hour, still unable to comprehend how Lizzie could've just up and left for the entire summer without so much as a simple farewell.

I was used to Emma being gone. She spent more time with her friends in Fairhaven or tending to her charities then she did at home. In fact, I wasn't sure she'd been home for more than a day or two in the past month. Mr. Borden didn't seem to mind. He often helped her pack, reminding her to take heed of the weather while stowing her wardrobe. Sometimes he even escorted her to the train. But he never assisted Lizzie, not even with the simple task of rigging her pole for fishing.

"Why do you think that is, love?"

Liam was digging for information. I knew for a fact he wasn't upset that Lizzie was gone, more likely felt relieved that I wouldn't be subjected to her mood swings and fits. But he didn't dare say that.

"'Tis you." The words came out before I had a chance to stop them, and Liam straightened up, set me away from him as he silently demanded an explanation.

"She wanted to meet you, and I refused. I did what you and Seamus are always telling me to and told her my private life was no concern of hers." I knew what I'd done was the right thing, but I felt guilty just the same. It wasn't like Lizzie was trying to be difficult, she just . . . was.

Liam tried to hide it, but I saw the small, smug smile that crept across his lips. I'd heard him talking to Seamus last week; he thought if Seamus expressed the same concerns as he did about my employment, then maybe I'd listen. Much to my displeasure, it had worked. Between the lot of them nettling me to put some space between myself and Lizzie, and all that Liam had said, I had made it clear to Lizzie I didn't want her to meet Liam. And she'd left, putting fifty miles and a summer's worth of space between us.

"Don't be getting all proud of yourself," I said as I wound my way back into his arms. "All your meddling did was land me alone with Mr. Morse, sharing the same tiny bit of attic space."

Liam tensed, his arms constricting around me to the point where I struggled to breathe. I could almost hear his warring head, the decision he was tossing around between staying put or charging over to the Bordens' house and pummeling Mr. Morse, a man he'd never even met, into the ground.

"Who is Mr. Morse?"

"He's Lizzie's uncle, her mother's younger brother."

Liam gave me a tight nod, not at all satisfied with my answer. What he wanted to know was what business Mr. Morse had here in Fall River, why he had any reason to keep in contact with the husband of a sister he'd lost almost thirty years ago, and why he was housed up in the attic with me.

"Mr. Borden and him are friends, I believe. He comes by often to visit with Lizzie and discuss the workings of the Bordens' farm in Swansea."

"So he and Lizzie are close?" Liam asked.

Liam was confused, and I didn't blame him. I'd lived in that house, watched Lizzie taunt her father with her idiosyncrasies while Mr. Borden firmly stood his ground. But it always ended in the same way—the mutual avoidance of each for days, sometimes weeks. And after watching the silent words that passed between John Morse and Abigail Borden in the guest room earlier today, I was certain she had a hand in his visits as well.

I thought about Liam's question for a moment. I'd seen John speaking to Lizzie many times, heard bits and pieces of their conversations, all revolving around Lizzie complaining about her father. He'd listen, never once disagreeing with her. In fact, the only time I'd ever heard him bite back was when Lizzie said something unbecoming about her stepmother. Even then, he didn't raise his voice, just softly reminded Lizzie that her stepmother too was subjected to Andrew Borden's harsh ways. And his bed. If anything, his presence made the house more hushed . . . more secretive.

"I'm not sure close is the right word," I said. "But he's around enough that they should be, I suppose."

"So he visits often?" Liam asked, and I shrugged my shoulders. No matter how hard I tried, I had yet to figure out Mr. Morse's visiting schedule. If I could, I'd have made sure the spare bedroom in the front of the house was made up and ready for his arrival rather than risk sharing the tiny attic with him.

"And he bothers you? Has he voiced an interest in you?" Liam asked.

I shook my head. Mr. Morse hadn't so much as laid a finger on me, never once uttered an inappropriate word. In truth, Mr. Morse had been nothing but a gentleman to me. But his proximity to me, the way he watched me like a hawk circling its prey, made me uneasy nonetheless.

"No. He treats me well enough, even tends to the wood in the cookstove and makes sure I have fresh water for the dishes. He will even do his own if I am still tending to the pots or salting what is left of the meat."

If it was possible, I'd just confused Liam more. I'd confessed my fear of a man who had done nothing but go out of his way to make sure I wasn't overburdened by his visits.

"He's a butcher; that's why I don't like him," I added.

Liam laughed, a full-on chuckle that had my whole body shaking right along with his. "What's so wrong with butchers?" he asked. "Back in Ireland, that was my trade. Seamus's too. I can have a lamb skinned and its carcass carved clean in a matter of minutes, and you seem to have taken a liking to me."

I had forgotten that Liam's father was a butcher and that he'd apprenticed under him, and would no doubt follow in the family business. But that was an entire ocean ago, back in Ireland when there was game to kill and meat to be had. Here, sitting on the front steps of his triple-decker house, listening to drunken verses of old songs ringing out from the windows, it all seemed like another life.

"So tell me, Liam, did your father bring his knives home?"

"The butcher shop was our home; it was nothing more than four rooms above and a small barn out back."

"Did you bring them with you when you went to visit friends? Did you carry a hatchet and a boning knife when you were visiting family or friends?"

He cocked his head, and I could guess what he was thinking. Sometimes he did. If they were going hunting, then yes, he'd pack his tools right alongside his gun. But if the visit was to consist solely of cards and ale, then no, he left them at home, locked up safely in the shop.

I didn't wait for him to answer. There was no game to be had in Fall River, no slaughtering of livestock going on in the Bordens' barn. There was absolutely no sound reason for Mr. Morse to be carrying his knives.

"I'm planning on visiting the Thompsons tomorrow to see if they still have a position open for a maid." I'd been toying with the idea for a few days now, ever since Liam planted the idea in my head. But until the words left my mouth just now, I hadn't realized I'd actually made the decision. "I won't be able to see you as much, and I doubt the pay will be as good, but . . . "

"I think that's a wise decision," Liam said when I trailed off.

"If they don't, then—"

"Then I'll see about getting you a job at the mill," Liam interrupted. "I'd rather see you there, working twice as hard for less money, than have you spend one more night in the Borden house."

Chapter 24

I rose two hours before dawn just to make sure my chores were done and I wouldn't be missed. I hadn't told the Bordens about my plan; I was quite sure they'd fire me on the spot for even considering a different employer. Plus, there was no use in borrowing trouble. I had no guarantee the position was even still open.

The steep hills of the Highland district flowed upward from the river, the large mansions towering over each other as if competing for space. I quickly looked down at the small piece of paper I had in my hand and read the address to myself for the hundredth time. I knew these streets, had walked them many a time during my brief employment with the Remingtons. I could tell you the quickest way to Corky Row from here, which pharmacist had the fairest prices, and which mill owner kept mistresses under the guise of maids. I knew if I took Rock Street to Walnut, I'd be there in less than ten minutes, but I didn't. Instead, I circled the streets as I tried to convince myself this was a good idea . . . the right thing to do.

The house was large—three stories of red brick, the attic alone boasting four dormered windows on each side. I thought about the two tiny windows in the front and back of the attic at the Borden house and how the airflow was stifled by the wall that divided the space into two sleeping quarters. The windows of this house and the fresh air blowing off the river would be a welcome change.

The shade of the pillared entryway offered a retreat from the midday sun, and I quickly walked up the steps, finally set in my resolve. The sweet sound of children laughing filtered out of an open window, followed by a swift but gentle reprimand. I barely had enough time to step back before the front door opened and two boys, barely old enough to be wearing britches, bounded out, one with a fishing pole the other with a handful of worms.

A woman appeared behind them, flustered but obviously happy. I couldn't help but smile. The life . . . the sheer joy I could feel pouring out of this house reminded me of home, of a life filled with warm smiles and simple pleasures. It reminded me of Cara.

"Sorry for that, my children . . . well, they tend to be a bit on the spirited side."

"They're boys," I said as if that was explanation enough; at least, that's the excuse my mum always had at the ready when my brothers came home skinned up and covered in mud.

"That they are." She smiled and tilted her head as if searching her memory for an engagement she had missed, one that involved me appearing on her doorstep.

"Sorry, ma'am. I didn't mean to trouble you, I was just wondering if you were still in need of a maid."

She looked me up and down, the small glint of happiness never leaving her eyes. "A maid? No. We filled that position a few weeks back, but as you can see, I'll be in need of a nanny in a few weeks' time . . . that is, if you think you can handle those two."

It was only then that I took her in, realized that I had been so fascinated with her pleasant demeanor that I failed to notice her expectant state. I didn't know much about birthing babies, but my guess was she was less than a few weeks away.

"Yes ma'am. I have two older siblings, seven younger, five of them boys."

I forced back the dark thoughts lingering in my mind as I spoke, the voice that told me I was the worst person she could hire for this job. I'd let my own mother down while I was watching Cara, dooming my baby sister to a life of hardship. Perhaps I hadn't done the right thing by coming here after all.

"Splendid," she said as she motioned me inside. "Why don't you step in out of this heat, and we'll have ourselves a proper talk."

I paused in the doorway, reminding myself that I'd been little more than a child myself when the accident happened. Besides, I was older, stronger, and more mature now. This job could be the best thing that ever happened to me, the thing that would help me bring Cara over to the States once and for all.

Our talk lasted over an hour, and not once did she ask my age, not once did she ask about my previous employers or why I had been discharged from their service. When I went to bring it up, to assure her that I was still in good standing with the Bordens, she waved me off, said she wouldn't concern herself with the gossip that circulated on "that side of town."

The conversation took longer than I expected, probably because we were interrupted every few minutes by a question from one of the maids or silly demands from the children. To say Mrs. Thompson ran her house loosely would not be a gross exaggeration, but I didn't care. The noise, the constant banter between the children, even the tiny dog sniffing around my feet, were all pleasant distractions from the realization of what I was doing . . . deserting Lizzie, leaving the suffering of that house behind.

I didn't have a firm offer of employment when I left, rather a promise that her husband would check my standing in the community and get back to me by the end of the week. But that didn't stop me from wondering, dreaming about what my new life in that house would be like. To live where you could actually open the windows, where children were encouraged to fish and dig for worms, where the mistress of the house actually spoke with her maids as opposed to simply leaving them lists.

Yes, leaving the Borden house was the right thing to do. The *only* thing to do.

Chapter 25

························ ✦ ························

I'd just walked in from the market, had a newsprint-wrapped piece of cod in my satchel along with some oysters and a few mussels the fishmonger had yet to sell. Neither was enough alone, but together I could stretch them into a fish stew that would last a day or two.

Mrs. Borden was standing by the front window, her hands curled around the bottom of the window sash as she forced it open, the ancient lace curtains fluttering in the afternoon breeze. She never did that, never let the natural light shine in or aired out the house. Instead, she kept it closed up tight, complaining that the noise and the road dust gave her a headache. I could only presume the change meant she was entertaining, perhaps her sister or a business associate of Mr. Borden's.

I walked around to the back of the house, my eyes looking out to the barn door. I couldn't help but wonder if Mr. Morse's tools were still there or if he'd brought them to his room for safer keeping. Somehow I couldn't get comfortable with either possibility. I just didn't trust Mr. Morse. Maybe if I got to know him better . . . but that would require my giving him a chance to explain himself and his peculiar behaviors, and that wasn't ever going to happen.

"Bridget, is that you?" Mrs. Borden called out as the spring latch on the kitchen door caught. Her words, gentle and meek, floated back from the front parlor. There was no fear of an intruder in her voice, no insistence that I show myself immediately.

"'Tis me, Mrs. Borden," I answered back as I set my daily purchases on the counter and reached for the kettle. It was still hot and sitting on the cookstove, empty. I filled it with water and placed it back on the stove. No doubt her guests would want more tea, and I'd be wise to have it at the ready.

I quickly grabbed my clean apron from the hook in the sink room and smoothed out whatever wrinkles I could as I headed towards her voice. Had I known she was expecting company, I would've done the marketing early, made sure the front parlor was dusted, and set out the good china she kept stored in the locked hutch. Slowing, I listened for other voices, trying to figure out who and how many were here from the conversation alone, but all I got was silence interrupted by street noise and the occasional chirp of a bird.

The front parlor was empty, not a soul in it save Mrs. Borden. No tray of tea and sweets, no business associates of Mr. Borden poring over paperwork or arguing over money. Not even Mr. Morse reading the daily paper as he rambled on about livestock breeding and crop rotation on the Borden's Swansea Farm.

I stood there in the doorway watching Mrs. Borden. She was seated by the window, her large frame barely fitting into the chair she'd dragged up to catch the breeze. I followed her line of vision through the leaded glass to the street beyond, curious as to what was holding her attention but saw nothing. Very rarely did she enter this room, preferring the more informal comfort of the sitting room. She came in here only to dust, leaving the larger duties for cleaning the windows and beating the rugs to me.

"You know I never sit in this room." She had to be speaking to me, but I turned around anyway and searched out the front entry for Mr. Borden. "It's a pleasant room, I suppose. Especially when the cool afternoon breeze blows through."

"It is," I lied, not wanting to contradict her. To be honest, I found the room cramped and impersonal, everything placed just so to give the illusion of wealth and power in a home too basic, too small, to be anything but ordinary. And that clock. I hated that clock. "May I get you something, Mrs. Borden? Perhaps some tea?"

She shook her head and turned around to look at me, an odd, almost sad smile parting her lips. "Sit with me, Bridget. For just a few minutes, sit with me."

She held out her hand when I didn't move, sweeping it in the direction of the small sofa opposite her. I sat down and dug myself deeper into the corner as I twisted my hands in my apron and waited for her to speak. Surely, she was preparing to chastise me for being late with my chores or for some error made to her morning meal. What I didn't expect was to be questioned about Lizzie.

"Lizzie left two days ago without so much as a goodbye to me or her father, but I presume you already know that."

I nodded as I tried to judge the tone of her voice. She didn't seem angry or even concerned, more relieved. My mind circled around the memory of the coins hidden in her hand the day Lizzie and Mr. Borden argued about the corset. It was such a simple gesture, one no one else had even noticed. But I'd seen it, and even now, I wondered exactly what it meant and if Mrs. Borden herself was just as misunderstood as Lizzie.

"Care to enlighten me as to what passed between you two?" Mrs. Borden asked.

I considered her question, was tempted to lie and tell her I wasn't privy to Lizzie's motives. Truth was, I had no idea why Lizzie had left so abruptly, but I'd assumed her stepmother did. The fact that she'd told no one—including her own father—that she was leaving, was even more reason to worry about her.

"She was angry with me, ma'am, upset that I wouldn't take her to meet my friend."

"Friend?" Mrs. Borden leaned forward in her chair, her eyes meeting mine as she read rather than listened to my answer. "This friend of yours wouldn't by chance be a boy."

I hung my head, my eyes tracing the intricate pattern on the rug as I mumbled my answer. "Yes, but I've never brought him here, Mrs. Borden. I know how Mr. Borden feels about male suitors, and I assure you, I have honored his wishes."

A faint smile softened her features. "Of course you have, I don't doubt that, Bridget. I would've heard of it had you not, from Mr. Borden if not Emma." She paused for a moment, her eyes glancing towards the window again before she whispered her next words as if musing to herself. "But Lizzie . . . I'm surprised she hasn't spoken about him, mentioned him to Mr. Borden in the hopes that he'd restrict your hours or threaten to remove you from his employment merely because your 'friend' exists."

Mrs. Borden got up from her seat, using the arms of the chair to help guide her heavy frame to a standing position. "Does Lizzie know his name?" she asked as she slowly made her way to the small table in the entryway where the morning post was left. She shifted through the pile of letters, coming up with one that looked hand delivered.

I watched as she placed it on the small table in front of the sofa, face down within inches of my hands, then answered her question. "Yes."

Mrs. Borden shook her head and took a seat next to me on the sofa. "It's not unusual for the mistress of the house to be close with her maid. Many a secret has passed between such confidants. I, myself, shared everything with my maid before I married Andrew. She was as close to me as my sisters, maybe more. But Lizzie is not the mistress of this house. I am, and she can't be trusted, not with your secrets nor your friendship."

I swallowed down my fear and forced myself to speak. The sooner this conversation was over, the better. "Is that what you wanted to speak to me about? Lizzie? I'm sorry if I overstepped—"

She held her hand up to silence me. I stopped speaking and shrank backwards, mindful that I had no place questioning Mrs. Borden. Andrew Borden was my employer, his wife his proxy.

"You've overstepped nothing, Bridget. It is Lizzie who I fear has taken advantage of you. I just wish you had come to me first and told me how unhappy you were here. I could have helped. John Morse could've helped."

I cringed at the sound of Mr. Morse's name. Little did Mrs. Borden know that I'd do nearly anything to avoid contact with him, would rather swallow down any displeasure than accept help from John Morse.

"I'm not unhappy," I went to say, but her attention cut to the message she'd left on the table, her eyes warning me not to lie.

"Do you know what that is?" she asked, and I almost picked the paper up and read it for myself. But it wasn't addressed to me. It wasn't even addressed to her. Andrew Borden's name was inked across the paper, the seal of the message broken.

"I know why you were up before dawn yesterday, scurrying around here to finish a day's worth of chores before breakfast. I also know you didn't get held up in town searching for just the right shade of gray muslin to mend Mr. Borden's pants."

She nudged the paper towards me, and I picked it up, my eyes glossing over as I took in the words scrawled across the paper.

"It's from Mr. Thompson. He's asking questions about why we dismissed you from our service, along with wanting to know your age and any complaints we wish to lodge against your name."

I swallowed hard, unsure of what to say, how to explain that I wasn't ungrateful for her and Mr. Borden's generosity, and ready to beg her not to fire me on the spot. But before I got the chance to say anything, she rose from her seat and plucked the message from my hands, returning it to the table in the entry hall without so much as a word in my direction.

Chapter 26

I stood up, fully prepared to quickly gather what few belongings I had and leave. It was preposterous to think I could apply for another job without the Bordens finding out.

Of course they'd found out. What I'd done was naïve and inexcusable; I should've been grateful I had a job at all, not go searching out something better.

Quickly, my mind raced through my options. I could go to the Thompsons and hope, pray, beg that she'd give me the job. But she didn't need me till the baby was born. How was I supposed to support myself for the next month?

Liam had mentioned working in the mill. I knew he made decent money. But even with the rent split six ways, he still struggled to pay his share and set some aside for our future. And wages for women were half that, not to mention the conditions were worse. Plus, where would I live? Being unmarried, sharing his place was unthinkable and would most certainly prevent me from securing any kind of respectable employment. My options were limited if not already gone.

"Please," I begged as I knotted my hand in my apron. "It was foolish and wrong of me to seek out the Thompsons. I know that now. I am truly grateful for all you have—"

She waved her hand in front of me, her plump fingers not-so-subtly instructing me to sit and remain silent. I did, not because

I wanted to, but because I needed this job. I needed *any* job. And if sitting quietly while I took the verbal lashing I had due meant I could keep it, then I'd gladly oblige.

"Have you mentioned this to Andrew or Lizzie yet?" she asked.

I shook my head. The last person I wanted to mention this to was Mr. Borden. And Lizzie . . . well, I'd purposely waited until she'd left to talk to the Thompsons.

Mrs. Borden sighed and dropped back down into the chair by the window. "You are not the first maid to leave, and I am quite sure I will be able to secure a replacement. Lizzie, however . . . I fear what she will do when she learns the news."

Her last words were whispered, more like a chilling thought she never intended to speak aloud than a statement requiring a response. But I answered anyway. "I can speak to Lizzie if you wish, tell her myself."

Mrs. Borden spun in her chair with a speed and determination unnatural for her girth. "You will do no such thing. For the sake of all of us damned to live in this house, you will do no such thing."

I'd never heard her raise her voice, never heard her mutter more than a whispered reminder to beat a rug or use more salt in the stew. Even in the few altercations I'd overheard between her and Lizzie, she'd stayed quiet, nodding or gently trying to redirect the conversation as Lizzie screeched at her about money or stealing her father's affections.

She sighed and collapsed back into the chair as if her tiny emotional outburst had sapped what little energy she had. "I tried to be a good mother to Lizzie. She was barely three, had little recollection of Sarah . . . of her mother. I knew it would take longer for Emma to accept me. She was older, knew and loved her mother, but Lizzie . . ." She paused, her eyes darkening as she physically shook off whatever memory had entrapped her soul. "Lizzie hasn't called me mother in years, won't even breathe my

Christian name. Mrs. Borden. She now refers to me coldly as Mrs. Borden."

I knew that; I'd witnessed it several times myself, but until this moment, until I saw the creases around Mrs. Borden's eyes and the heavy set of her shoulders, I hadn't realized how much it pained her. Not once had I considered that this woman might actually care. Maybe that's where my words came from—an overwhelming response to the pain I saw echoed in her eyes.

"I can stay, Mrs. Borden. If you think it would be easier for Lizzie, then I can stay on here."

"No," she said, her usual meek demeanor back in place. "You're not the first maid Lizzie has taken a liking to, but you are younger and perhaps a bit naïve. She knows that, has gained your trust and made you feel important, like you had a friend . . . a sister in this new world."

I nodded, curious as to where she was going with this. "She's been kind to me, ma'am."

"Kind." She repeated the word back to me, but it didn't sound so harmless coming from her.

She got up and pulled a key from her dress pocket and bent down to the bottom drawer of the hutch. Her hands trembled and it took her two tries to fit the tiny key into the lock. The drawer scraped open, and I watched her sift through the fine linens she kept stored in there until she came up with a small, clear pot.

"Do you know what this is?" she asked.

I took the small jar from her hand and uncorked the lid. I didn't need to bring it to my nose to know. The smell was so strong, the bitter, almost almondlike scent giving it away.

"Prussic acid," I said as I recapped the jar and handed it back to her.

"The maid you replaced—Katie—she was a bit older than you and had been here in Fall River for quite some time. She knew the rumors that circulated about us and took the position anyway.

Lizzie took a liking to her, as she has you, but Katie was married, set in her ways with no need for companionship. For months, Lizzie tried to pull her in. She helped her with the chores, would shun her charities in favor of going to the market for Katie, even went so far as to demand that Mr. Borden give her more than one day off a week. But Katie wanted none of it, told Lizzie she was capable of minding her own matters and didn't need her interfering."

I thought back to the last few weeks . . . the last few months. Lizzie was always helping me out, even if it meant just sitting there in the kitchen keeping me company as I cooked or washed the dishes. I knew even then it was improper, but I missed my home, my friends, even Liam on the days he picked up extra shifts. Her idle prattle soothed my mind. There was no way around it; I enjoyed Lizzie's company, probably would have chosen it even if I wasn't so lonely.

"Katie fell ill last fall. We all presumed it was exhaustion, but eventually her stomach turned on her, leaving her huddled over her bedpan for days on end. At Andrew's insistence, I let her go. I gave her enough money to carry her through the month and then found her another job. She works for my sister now, hasn't missed a day of work due to illness since leaving this house."

I followed her gaze to the tiny bottle she still grasped in her hand. She didn't speak her next words; she didn't need to. I knew what she was implying, knew what she rightfully feared.

"Do you recall a few months back when someone broke into the barn?" she asked, and I nodded. I knew for a fact it hadn't been broken into, that it was Lizzie pilfering things from her own father. "I begged Andrew to call the police, but he insisted on looking around himself first, seeing what, if anything, was taken."

"And?" I asked, trying to coax her along. I knew there were a few axe marks marring the back of the barn door, and that it appeared as if someone had tried to pry the lock off his trunk, but

Mr. Borden never filed an official report, never so much as had the police question the local street kids.

"He found this," she said, her hand shaking around the tiny glass bottle. "It was hidden beneath a sack of seed for the pigeons."

I couldn't still the shiver that burrowed through my core. The only one who loved those pigeons, the only one that ever fed or cared for them, was Lizzie.

"Are you saying that . . ." I couldn't even finish the thought. The idea of Lizzie doing such a hateful thing was impossible.

"I don't know what to think anymore, Bridget. I will speak with Mr. Thompson and explain to him the misfortune we have in losing you. I've no plans to tarnish your name and will tell them that it is I who has asked you to leave, that I feel John Morse has taken an interest in you that is inappropriate."

I paled at her words. The excuse she planned to give them would indeed impair me, not to mention it was wholly untrue. It wasn't even sound. Mr. Morse lived in another town, came into Fall River at odd hours. His behavior may have been peculiar, but he certainly had never propositioned me. "But that's not . . . he never . . . I never . . ."

Mrs. Borden chuckled at my inability to form a coherent sentence. The sound had me stopping abruptly as I strained to hear it again. It was pleasant, jovial, and I couldn't help but wonder when the last time she laughed was.

"Fear not, my dear Bridget. I've become quite adept at spinning assumptions and family history to my favor. I will assure Mr. Thompson that you have been nothing but proper and loyal in your work here." She stopped for a moment, her laughter returning. "Plus, nobody in Fall River truly knows John Morse and the same goes for him of them. He won't suffer as a result of this white lie, and I can assure you, *you* won't, either."

We sat there in silence for a few moments, her staring at her hands, me wondering whether or not her entire plan would work.

It wasn't until the clock announced the top of the hour that I got up. Sitting here, waiting for one of us to speak, was making me anxious, my mind traveling a series of what-ifs as I replayed every conversation, every passing gesture between Lizzie and me.

"Bridget," Mrs. Borden called after me, and I stopped right there in the doorway. "I will write it all down on paper for you, the reference and reasoning behind your dismissal, just in case the Thompsons refuse you employment. You can use my written reference to secure a position somewhere else. In exchange, may I ask a favor of you?"

I turned around then, surprised to see her still staring at her hands, not bothering to glance up and acknowledge me. "Yes ma'am?"

"Lizzie is gone for the remainder of the summer. From what I understand, she will be visiting friends with Emma. I originally intended to ask that you remain here until she returns, but I now realize how unfair that would be of me. You have suffered enough already. I will ask that you stay at least two more weeks, however. I have some things I need to attend to, and I fear your sudden departure would put Mr. Borden in a questioning mood."

"Of course, ma'am," I said as I turned to walk away. Right then, I think I would've agreed to anything just to get out of that room, away from the horrid implications that even I could no longer dismiss.

"And one more thing, Bridget. I'll address this matter with Andrew in my own time. You must keep it to yourself for now."

Chapter 27

With Lizzie gone and Mrs. Borden tucked into the guest room attending to some seams in one of her summer dresses, I quietly made my way down the back stairs. With everything I'd learned today, I needed to see Liam. He'd sort through this for me, remind me that nothing mattered so long as we had each other.

The house was dark, the candle Abigail Borden had left lit in the front window filtering through the rooms. She knew I was going out, even knew I was planning on meeting Liam. Her only word of caution had been to make sure he walked me home. Apparently, the streets of Fall River were no place for a young lass to be wandering about alone.

Her concern warmed my heart. It made me think of my own mother back in Ireland, and then the mother Lizzie had lost. I'd seen a new side of Mrs. Borden today, the quiet worry she harbored for the girls. She seemed willing to do anything and everything to keep them safe, but Lizzie didn't see that, or as her stepmother had put it, *Lizzie's excitable nature prevented her from seeing it.*

I made my way through the kitchen to the sitting room, was nearly clear across the room before a subtle intake of breath startled me. I quickly darted into the parlor and grabbed the lit candle from the window and held it up to confirm who I saw.

I watched Mr. Borden for a moment, his hand tracing tiny circles across the mantel, each mindless movement carefully

22

skirting around the brass key he kept there. I knew he saw me, the flare of light and my not-so-gentle steps had given me away. But he made no movement towards me, uttered no words of acknowledgment, not even a curt nod of the head.

I put the candle down on the table in the sitting room. The narrow staircases in this house could be treacherous in the dark, and I saw no wick or flame in his hand.

"Do you know why I lock my bedroom door at night? Why my desk, and Abigail's wardrobe closet, even the china hutch housing my family's silver, are all locked each day?" he finally asked, his words coming on top of a heavy sigh.

It wasn't just the chests he kept locked, but everything. Every door, every window, every crevice of this house was sealed off with an iron key. And each night he tested them, over and over as if to make sure nobody had tampered with them. I could still hear the sound echoing through the walls of the house, the sharp, metallic smack of the lock sliding into place and then being undone again, and redone. It was like a ritual, a routine. God knows why he did it or how long it would last, but if I'd learned anything in that house, it was to pretend I saw and heard nothing.

"Prowlers, sir?" I asked, knowing full well that he wasn't afraid of the occasional hooligan. To be honest, the people in this town were too afraid of him and his "spinster" daughters to even think about entering this house unannounced.

I saw the slight nod of his head in the glow of the candlelight. "Yes, prowlers. Thieves on the inside."

I knew what he meant; he believed the items stolen from him were Lizzie's doing. That's probably why he hadn't summoned the police immediately when the barn was broken into. He alerted the police only *after* he'd searched the barn himself. That was probably a not-so-subtle cue to Lizzie that he was in control. That he believed her to be the culprit and that he would no longer tolerate her behavior. Fortunately for her, he found the prussic acid before the police arrived.

"I owe you an apology, Miss Sullivan."

He turned to look at me then, and even from across the room, I could see the sincerity in his eyes, the strength and humility it took for him to utter those words. Sorry wasn't a word I'd ever heard used in this home before, the words "my due" and "my right" often taking its place.

"I shouldn't have let this go on for as long as I have. I knew Lizzie had taken a liking to you and purposely ignored it. For that, I am truly sorry. With you occupying Lizzie's thoughts, with her every action centered around you, Abigail and Emma had a reprieve, a brief chance to resume the semblance of a normal life. I selfishly wanted that for them and turned a blind eye to the unnatural fascination Lizzie has towards you."

"No need to apologize, sir. I am under your employ . . ." I went to say, but he cut me off.

"Under my employment and, as such, under my protection." His voice rose now, and I got a small understanding of how his business associates must feel and why he was so successful. His tone brooked no rebuttal, not even a hint that an alternate explanation was warranted or welcomed.

"My first wife, Sarah . . . Lizzie's mother, was a good woman, a good mother. She struggled with demons, but she always won. As each of my children approached their first birthdays, I could see the demons lifting, the spirit I fell in love with slowly coming back."

I'd heard rumors of such demons, seen them firsthand back in Ireland. Maggie O'Shea lived only a few miles away. She married my oldest brother Sean when she was barely sixteen. I had a niece, a round little thing with a shocking head of black hair. I remember Sean bringing her by the house for days at time, claiming Maggie had birthing fever and was out of sorts and talking nonsense. Even when the fever broke, Maggie seemed different—always crying, always mumbling to herself. I couldn't help but wonder how Maggie was now, if she had borne my brother more children, or if the demons Mr. Borden spoke of had taken her mind, too.

"My Uncle Laddy's wife struggled with them as well, but she was weak, let her sickness claim not only her soul but the souls of her children as well. That's why I did it. That's why I killed the pigeons, Miss Sullivan."

I paled, my mind floating back to the image of Lizzie's pets, mangled and headless. It had taken me hours to clear the crimson from the kitchen floor, the knots of the wood absorbing it, the color spreading through the rough grain of the wood all while the smell of blood pudding festered in the air.

"I'm sorry, sir?" I didn't understand how slaughtering Lizzie's pets had anything to do with his first wife's death or how he could possibly justify what he'd done that day.

"Lizzie may not be a handsome woman, and no one, maid or master, has escaped the gossip that surrounds her. Regardless of how we live, no matter how much I try to portray this family as miserly and cheap, the enormity of my wealth is known. One day that wealth will pass on to my daughters. Any prosperity-seeking man would be more than willing to overlook Lizzie's peculiarities in the hopes of securing her hand and in turn, my money. I cannot let that happen."

"But there are no suitors, sir. I am sure Lizzie would have told me if there were."

Mr. Borden shook his head and took a step closer, the same pity I'd heard earlier in Mrs. Borden's voice when she'd shown me the prussic acid now mirrored in his expression. "You are young yet, Miss Sullivan, too young to decipher reality from fiction, to understand the things Lizzie *chooses* to tell you are not always true. There are young men, one in particular. My associates have seen Lizzie talking to him in town. I've heard his voice myself in the barn. He delivered the feed for her birds once a month, but she meets him nearly every week in town."

"But Lizzie married to a man of good standing . . . isn't that what you want?" *Isn't that what every father wanted?* I added to myself. That is why I was sent here, why my own parents gave me what little money they had to buy my passage. They wanted a better life for me, one with a good man with a solid reputation.

"Most fathers would want that, yes. I mourn the loss of the grandchildren I will never know, the name and wealth that will never be passed on. But I would gladly give away all my wealth and position if it meant not passing the illness that curses this family on to my grandchildren." He straightened up and looked me in the eyes. "I'll keep Lizzie alone until the day I die, if that's what it takes to keep this curse from consuming another generation."

My memories circled around that night, around the story Lizzie had told me the evening I'd found her wandering the kitchen in her day clothes. Andrew Borden's great-aunt, the one who'd dropped her own children into the well. She was the one he was referring to, the illness he was desperately trying to avoid. Lizzie swore her mother suffered the same madness, was convinced it was afflicting her as well. I struggled to swallow as I remembered Lizzie's face in the pale glow of my lantern as I tucked her in, how she confessed she was afraid the curse was coming for her. Blood or marriage . . . it didn't matter; anybody who bore the Borden name was cursed in her mind.

She wasn't the only one who was afraid of that. Her father was, too. And he planned to keep Lizzie a spinster her whole life to avoid it.

Chapter 28

"I can't believe it. I can't believe it was that easy," Liam said, pouring a spot of whiskey. "You were so worried, and I thought there was a chance I was going to have to come over there and tell them myself."

He handed me the glass, and I sniffed it, nearly keeling over at the biting smell. I hated the smell of whiskey, always had, but being from Cork had sealed my fate years ago. Any celebrating there was to be done began and ended with whiskey.

"To the most beautiful girl in all of Fall River—to Bridget!" Liam shouted, raising his glass high above his head. He drank it and slammed the glass back down on the table, tossing me a sloppy, carefree smile. Watching him like this—celebrating and worry free—made me wonder how long he'd been waiting for me to leave. How many nights he'd hovered on Second Street long after he dropped me off, and how many times he'd warred with himself over me working there.

"I wouldn't say it was *easy*. I've not told Mr. Borden yet."

"Why not?" Liam asked as he wrapped his arm around my waist and pulled me close. "Haven't you got to give him some time to replace you?"

I nodded. I should have told him, but Mrs. Borden seemed so insistent that I keep it to myself. Besides, the only time I would have been able to bring it up it just didn't feel right, not when Mr. Borden was so upset about Lizzie. He'd spoken more to me in those ten minutes than he had the entire time I'd worked there, and it shocked me. Hearing him confess about the pigeons and apologize for saddling me with Lizzie took the wind out of me, made me completely forget about my new post.

"Thompsons, eh?" Seamus downed another shot and pulled Minnie close. "Sounds right fancy to me." He made his way down her neck, kissing and nipping like they were the only two in the room. Minnie laughed loudly, hiccupping as he stopped at her neckline.

I snuck a glance at Liam, his bright blue eyes and strong hands reminding me of our future—our plan to eventually get out of Fall River and get married. It couldn't come fast enough. Leaning into him, I smiled as he dropped a kiss to the top of my head.

"I'll stay on at the Borden house a couple more weeks. Mrs. Borden needs me and with Lizzie gone . . . well, things seem calmer, quieter," I said.

"For what?" Liam asked, pulling me in for another quick peck. He grinned when I kissed him back, a broad smile that reached his eyes. "Can't she just get a replacement now? Let you spend the rest of your summer in a house that's not so damn bleak?"

I heard the frustration in his voice; I knew that me working for the Bordens had taken its toll on him, too. "Lizzie's gone for the whole summer anyway. Emma, too. It's just Mr. and Mrs. Borden. Besides, the Thompsons don't need me just yet."

I didn't exactly know why Mrs. Borden needed me to stay for two more weeks, but I figured it was the least I could do, given that I was leaving them without a proper replacement.

Minnie leaned in close, swayed on her feet before grasping hold of the table to keep herself steady. I knew what she was doing, what she wanted to hear. Gossip. I thought back to Mrs. Borden's soft voice, Mr. Borden's furrowed brow, and his constant fear for Lizzie. It was bad enough they'd gotten saddled with a daughter they needed to watch like a hawk; they most certainly didn't deserve to be talked about for it.

"I was wrong about them. They're not at all like I thought. They're kind."

Seamus looked at me like I'd sprouted horns and become the devil himself. "Kind? Isn't a man or woman in Fall River that would call that man kind! Miserly maybe, odd, and perhaps a bit insane . . . but kind?"

"Yes, kind!" I bit back, relaxing only when I felt Liam's arms wrap around me. The slight scruff of his jaw rubbed against my cheek, and I smiled. He always found a way to moderate things between Seamus and me.

"You don't know what it's like in that house." I felt the tears stinging at the edges of my eyes and blinked them back, frustrated with myself. I should be celebrating, not crying.

"Hey, don't cry, love. Please. It's over now." Liam's voice fell to a barely audible level, soft and gentle, as he pulled me deep into his chest. "You did everything you could for her, you know that, right?"

"For who? What the hell are you talkin' about?" Seamus asked, and Liam waved him off. Seamus grumbled something, then grabbed Minnie's hand and stumbled into the next room, coming back for a split second only to grab the whiskey bottle I'd hidden.

The tears falling weren't even tears of sadness, but rather tears of exhaustion. A year of trying to navigate that family, of trying to pacify Lizzie and protect her from the world. I hadn't realized it at the time, but it was draining.

"I'm not sure I'll even get a chance to explain to her. By the time she comes back, I'll be gone." I had purposely avoided thinking about that day and the hurt I was causing her, the promise I was breaking. I thought about leaving her a note, explaining to her my reasoning, but what was I going to say . . . that her meddling, her father's dark moods, the insanity that seemed to strangle this home, were too much for even me to bear? At the end of the day, I was leaving her alone here to fend for herself.

"That's the kindness in you talkin'," Liam soothed. "You've got to remember that she's a grown woman. She'll be fine."

"She's less of a grown woman than I am," I hiccupped out, folding myself deeper into his arms. "She's soft and doesn't understand what her parents are doing. Without me, I don't know what she'll do."

I felt the deep rise and fall of Liam's chest beneath me. He lifted my chin and met my eyes with his. "Whatever happens to that woman is no worry of yours from this point on, understand?"

He put me aside, stood up, and walked over to the mattress on his side of the room. I stared at him blankly, wondering if this was the moment I'd always expected would come. After all, we were in his flat, in his room, and there was no one around to see. No one to think we were being improper.

Liam caught the twitch of concern in my eyes and smiled, his eyes twinkling like they did when he was up to mischief. "Ah, not yet. Not here. Not until I find you a proper home, with a proper bed." Instead of lying down, he lifted the ratty mattress, gently slid aside the sheet wrapped around it and pulled out a wrinkled envelope.

"Open it," he said, pressing it into my hands.

I slid the top open, gasping at what I saw. Money. A whole stack of it. I ran my finger across the bills' worn edges, stunned into silence.

"I told you I've been saving. We're almost there. *Almost*. Six months at the Thompsons should do it, Bridget. We'll be able to leave here, just you and me. Start over somewhere else, somewhere they don't know us and don't care where we came from, someplace where your sister Cara will be safe and happy."

I smiled at him, my heart swelling more with each word he uttered. I had no idea whether there even was a place like that, but I didn't care. As long as I was with Liam, nothing else would matter. Not Andrew Borden. Not his wife. Not the countless sleepless nights I'd spent in that house nor the chiming of that horrible clock in the parlor. Not even Lizzie.

Chapter 29

The heat didn't bother me that morning. It was still humid, the steam rising from the road the instant the sun came up. But somehow everything seemed lighter, less stifling. I slipped down the back stairs, anxious to start my morning duties. I wanted to go to town and see if I could get a stronger thread to help Mrs. Borden with her mending. I talked to her about stitching together a new dress; she had gotten bigger lately and the seams of the few dresses she owned tugged no matter how tightly she laced her corset. But Mrs. Borden wouldn't hear of it. She insisted that minor repairs were all that were needed. I doubted it would work, but I could understand her desire to try.

I stopped on the landing of the second floor and stared at the wooden door that led to Mr. Borden's bedroom. Recently he'd taken to entering his and Mrs. Borden's bedroom from the front of the house, passing through Lizzie's room on his way. The bed Lizzie had wedged against the door connecting their rooms had been moved yesterday, the rug that covered her floor beaten and lain back down. And with Lizzie gone for the remainder of the summer, I wondered if he'd open his door to the hallway even once. Air it out.

I paused a few steps from the bottom, the smell of coffee and jam greeting me. I knew for a fact Mr. and Mrs. Borden were still in their chambers; I'd heard their quiet whisperings as I stood outside their room, shamelessly bending my ear towards their door. Mr. Borden was asking his wife about her plans for the day, suggesting that perhaps she go visit her sisters for tea. Mr. Morse was gone as well; he'd left yesterday without so much as a word of his departure. That could only mean . . .

There was no need to announce my arrival. I knew she was waiting for me, had probably had her eyes trained on the small hall that led to the back staircase since the moment she got back. Lizzie was sitting at the kitchen table alone, her lips upturned into a tiny, apathetic grin. She'd been gone four days with no word, not even a goodbye, and yet there she was, smiling like all was forgiven.

"Miss me, Bridget?" Lizzie slowly stirred her coffee, her gaze caught in the tiny circular motions.

I walked past her, giving her nothing more than a sideways glance as I went about preparing the morning meal.

"Oh, come now," Lizzie continued. "You can't stay upset with me forever."

I could. Lizzie knew exactly what she was doing and how she was affecting me. It was bad enough having to look for new employment behind her back, but having her show up out of thin air, all but taunting me, was much, much worse.

"I see my father moved my bed," she said, and I didn't have the heart to tell her it was me and Mrs. Borden who had done it, that her stepmother was hoping to open the windows in both the front and the back of the house to air it out.

"Your father said you were gone for the summer, that you were going to stay with Emma and her friends in Fairhaven."

Lizzie took a deep breath, then said, "Well, I couldn't exactly leave you alone with my father for the entire summer, now could I?" She paused and stared at me, her eyes lifting as if she was waiting for an answer. Knowing her, she expected some sort of confirmation or warped thank-you. But I had no idea what she was talking about, and I was still hurt that she had left without saying goodbye.

"You know he sold Mrs. Borden a half-stake in the house on Fourth Street?" she continued when I didn't answer.

I nodded; I hadn't been privy to that argument. It happened over five years ago. Long before I was under the Bordens' employ, long before I was even in the States. But everybody in Fall River knew about it, talked about it as if it had just happened yesterday. Mr. Borden had given his wife a share in the property her sisters lived in, sending Lizzie into a fit. Both she and Emma argued that it was unfair of their own father to look more favorably upon his second wife than his own daughters.

For once, Mr. Borden had relented, more interested in keeping his image intact than standing his ground with Lizzie. "Yes, and to make amends, didn't he give you and Emma the family house off Ferry Street, the one you were born in?"

"Not gave," Lizzie fired back. "Sold."

The contempt was evident in her eyes, in the hollow look just behind the pain. Mr. Borden was certainly not a charitable man, but he made sure his family had what *he* thought they needed. Granted, Lizzie thought she deserved more, but she never went without the necessities.

Ignoring the irritation in her voice, I calmly responded, "For one dollar, Lizzie. That's little more than the cost of a new corset."

She laughed and reached for a cookie. "And did I tell you what we did?" she asked, not giving me a chance to respond before continuing. "Just last week, we sold it back to him for twenty-five hundred dollars apiece."

I shook my head and fought off the urge to tell Lizzie how greedy I thought that was. Where I came from, you didn't profit off family; you looked after them, tended to their needs the best you could.

"Why would you do that?" I asked.

"You know Father is a wealthy man, equal in station to the Garners and the Masons, yet we live here."

"Here?" I questioned. I knew the Bordens' house wasn't as grand as the Remingtons' or the Thompsons' or any of the other homes on the Hill, but it was cleaner than the mill houses most of my friends lived in, and practically a mansion compared to the three-room flat Liam was hoping to build us.

"We live on the same street as a Chinese laundry," Lizzie said as she shifted in her chair, loosening the tight neckline of her dress. "The horse teams keep me up at night, and the street peddlers crowd the way. We don't even have a water closet or electric lights."

I could do without the electric lights, but a better ice chest would be nice. I looked over at the day-old mutton stew I'd left sitting on the cookstove overnight. Mrs. Borden had helped me prepare it last night and the thick, meaty smell still clung to everything. It hadn't been good the first time, and I doubted it would be any better after I flavored it.

"I sold the house back to him for you, Bridget."

I stumbled back at the sad betrayal in her voice. "What?"

Lizzie sighed. Her eyes flitted to the back door. I'd left the milk and ice pans out, but they were still empty, the delivery boy probably slowed down by the heat. "I'm sorry I left you here, Bridget. That was wrong of me. But I can't just stay here and wither away, and I won't let you either."

I thought about telling her right then about my new position with the Thompson family. I'd planned on telling her, eventually. I figured I'd ask Mrs. Thompson for a morning off and come back here, tell Lizzie why I did it, and promise to always be her friend. I could do that now. There was nothing stopping me, save the certainty that she'd ask me to stay and the fear that I'd relent and say yes.

"There was enough money in my father's safe to get you to Swansea, but I got to thinking that Swansea wasn't far enough, that somehow his reach would extend there, too," Lizzie said. "But the money from the house, now that's enough to buy you passage back to Ireland, and set up a proper home for your family and that sister you're always talking about."

Chapter 30

I tossed a bay leaf into the cast-iron pot and stirred it under, watching as the green leaf faded to gray and then black as the water drained it of its flavor. Of its very essence. I couldn't help but think of Lizzie in that moment, of who she might have been before I came to work here. Surely there was a time she wasn't so paranoid, so determined to protect herself from invisible enemies. Perhaps that spark of life had been leached out of her too, drained away until the only thing left was this husk of a woman, tired, afraid, and angry at the world.

Lizzie had left minutes ago, had simply gotten up and walked out the back door without another word. I didn't want her or Emma's money nor did I understand why she was so convinced I might need it. Or why she thought her father meant me harm.

"Good morning, Bridget," Mrs. Borden said as she walked into the kitchen. She looked happier, more rested than I'd seen her in weeks. "I see you are fixing my stew."

She smiled as she reached for the loaf of bread and pot of jam in the middle of the table. My guess was she thought I'd put it there; she probably had no idea that Lizzie was back.

"Yes, ma'am. I figured I'd better get a head start on it."

"No need," she said. "Andrew said he would stop by the fishmonger's on the way home from his morning business. I was thinking oyster soup."

"I can get them," I said, not bothering to turn around. "I was going to stop by the Five and Ten to pick up some thread for your dresses anyway."

She caught the darkened tone of my voice and rose from her chair, came over to stand beside me, stilled my stirring hand as she spoke. "Bridget? Something wrong?"

I shook my head, not wanting to tell her the truth. There'd been a lightness to her step when she came down the stairs this morning, and I didn't want to take that away from her.

"Nothing, ma'am. I'm tired, 'tis all."

"It's the heat," she said as she sat back down and fanned herself with her hand. "It needs to break soon or we'll all succumb to exhaustion, I fear."

It wasn't the heat she needed to fear, but Lizzie. Something had happened in the wee morning hours to bring her home, and I doubted she'd made it into this house unnoticed. My guess was that Mr. Borden knew she'd returned.

"And don't worry about anything," Mrs. Borden continued. "Least of all the position you want at the Thompsons'. I put a good word in for you and asked them to kindly grant me two weeks to find a replacement. Everything is going to end up just fine."

Mrs. Borden smiled, actually looked happy. I hadn't seen her this pleasant, this relaxed ever, and I knew beyond a shadow of a doubt that any peace she'd found would dissolve the second she learned Lizzie was home.

"This is a new start for you, Bridget. A new start for you and me both."

I nodded, wondering what new start of her own she was referring to. I was leaving. I was the one with plans and a future with Liam. She was still stuck here, tending to Mr. Borden's needs while sidestepping Lizzie's volatile moods.

"Did you want me to tend to your mending?" I asked, hoping that settling into the mundane chores of the day would take my mind off the upheaval I could feel patiently waiting to descend on this house.

"No need. I think today I'll spend some time with my sisters. The mending can wait."

I nodded, not sure whether I was relieved or upset. Having her out of the house would give me time to talk to Lizzie, figure out why she was back and what she had planned. But that meant I'd be alone, in this house, with a person who, right now, I didn't trust.

Mrs. Borden left the room, mumbling something about a new bolt of fabric she'd seen downtown. She'd all but torn up the second-floor guest room, covered it so densely with thread, fabric, and buttons I couldn't make heads or tails of anything. My guess was she'd tinker around in there a bit with her sewing, then call on her sisters.

● ● ●

I rarely went into the Bordens' bedroom. Mrs. Borden took care of cleaning it herself, even emptied and rinsed out their chamber pot each morning. But I needed to talk to Mr. Borden, and I was tired of waiting for him to come to me.

It would've been easier to go up the back stairs, but I purposely went up the main staircase, wanting a reason to cut through Lizzie's room to get to his. Her bed was still made, not even a wrinkle on the quilt. The bag she'd left with was wedged underneath her writing desk, as if she were trying to hide it. I wondered what time she'd gotten back and how long she'd been sitting in the kitchen waiting for me. If my instincts were right, it was longer than I wanted to know.

I had to skirt around Lizzie's bed to get to the connecting door. I tested the handle, already knowing it was locked. I knocked once on the door and heard the gruff mumbling of a curse as Mr. Borden shuffled across the room. Even during daylight, when the house was active and the streets busy, Mr. Borden locked himself inside that room.

The lock finally slid open, the door opening just enough for his eyes to meet mine. "Bridget?" he questioned.

"She's back, sir." I stepped aside, sweeping my hand out to the leather travel bag hidden behind her desk chair. "I saw her this morning in the kitchen."

He nodded once, short and tight, then stepped out of the bedroom, locking the door behind him. He didn't look surprised or even concerned. "Is she home now?"

"No, sir," I replied.

"Good." He picked up Lizzie's bag and set it on her bed. He was oddly careful with her things, taking them out one by one and searching each garment by hand before he laid it out and patted it down again. He slid open the clasp of Lizzie's weathered coin purse, quickly shook out the contents into his palm, and pushed around the money as if counting it. In one swift move, he'd separated out several coins and slid all but two into his own pocket. "I spoke with her briefly last night."

I was curious as to what words had passed between them and why I hadn't heard Mr. Borden's raised voice or Lizzie's stomping feet. There was only one kind of argument that I knew of that played out in silence, and it never ended well.

"See to it that you find me when Lizzie returns." He finished placing the items back in Lizzie's bag, apparently content in what he'd found, or more accurately, *not* found. He closed the bag and took care to place it in the exact same spot it had been sitting in before, even adjusted the angle of the desk chair until it was just right.

I nodded, quite aware he couldn't see me as he headed down the front stairs. I had no intention of being here when Lizzie came home. If Lizzie found out that I'd spoken to her father, there would be hell to pay. And I had no intention of being here when she realized someone had taken money from her, either. Mr. Borden had left her barely enough for a piece of candy, never mind enough for another train ticket out of Fall River. I'd reckoned she wouldn't be happy to discover she was even more trapped now than she had been before.

Chapter 31

The Smiths owned the largest pharmacy in Fall River. Every son had some stake in the business, each of their wives always hovering about, trying to catch wind of what little bits of misfortune they could. They'd spread the gossip around—hushed whispers after Sunday services, secretive conversations over tea—always denying their involvement in any such conduct whenever asked. Mr. Borden had warned me to keep my mouth shut in there. His family was no stranger to the Smiths' gossip-addled minds, and I doubted he wanted me adding to his troubles.

The bell above the door jingled as I walked in, alerting every wandering eye to my arrival. Usually, I went to Gallagher's pharmacy on the Hill, but after Lizzie's outburst there a few weeks back, I thought it best to come here instead.

I kept my head down and made my way to the counter, ignoring the group of youngsters sitting at the soda fountain. It was Saturday, and they were all gathered around the counter, marbles in hand, as they sucked down what would've cost a day's pay back home. Soon they'd be out front, crowding the sidewalk as they played.

I saw Eli Bence in the back corner, restocking one of the shelves. I'd always liked him, appreciated his honesty and kind face. Despite the fact that I rarely came into the store when I wasn't rushed or weary from running errands, the clerk always had a smile for me, always called me by my rightful name. It was folks like him who made living in Fall River bearable, almost pleasant.

Eli smiled when his eyes met mine and he waved me over. "Mornin', Bridget, what brings you in here today?"

I need a bottle of Mrs. Pinkham's vegetable oil," I whispered, hoping nobody but Eli heard me. It wasn't for me, it was for Mrs. Borden and the hot flashes she said interrupted her sleep, but I blushed nonetheless.

He took it down off the shelf and wrapped it in paper before placing it in a bag. "Anything else?"

I shook my head. There was a bottle of Crab Apple Blossom perfume sitting on the glass counter that I knew Liam would like, but I did not have the money to waste. "A bottle of peppermint oil," I said, hoping that would work just as well.

"How's your brother Peter doing?" I asked as I counted out my coins. Liam hadn't mentioned him since the night of the prayer vigil, and I'd forgotten to ask about him.

"He's well. Liam was by to see him yesterday, said he'd continue to cover his shifts 'til the spell passed."

The spell he was talking about was scarlet fever, and I doubted it would simply just pass. Liam had fallen ill as a child back in Ireland, and thus was one of Peter's few visitors. Liam had gotten better, gone on with his life like the fever never happened, but for every boy like him, there were three others who died. The extra shifts were a blessing more than a favor, a way for us to move up our plans for building our own home and bringing Cara to the States.

"I'll keep him in my prayers," I said as I looped my drawstring bag around my wrist and picked up my purchases. I still had to pick up the thread for Mrs. Borden's mending so I didn't have much time to chat. Plus, Eli had an odd look on his face, almost like he pitied me for some reason. I didn't like people looking at me like that, not even Liam's friends.

"Bridget," he called after me as I turned to leave. He'd tossed his apron down on the counter and gave a knowing nod to one of the other sales clerks before making his way towards me. "Walk with me for a bit."

"I can't," I said and looked around. The respectable people of Fall River may not have known I was spoken for, but three other maids I could see just outside did. The last thing I wanted was word getting back to Liam that I'd been flirting with someone else. Plus, Eli was married, had been for a few years.

Eli smiled, took me by the elbow, sat me down at the far end of the soda fountain, and handed me a tonic. He shook his head when I went for my coin purse, and nudged the glass in my direction, waiting for me to take a sip.

"Lizzie was in here this morning," he started in, and I nearly coughed up what little I had managed to swallow. When she'd left today, she headed for the barn. I'd presumed that's where she still was, tinkering with her fishing line or checking the weight of her sinkers.

"It was early," Eli said, seeing my confusion. "I'd yet to unlock the door. She was waiting for me when I arrived."

I quickly ran through the times in my head. It was six-thirty when I came down to start the morning meal. I knew for a fact that Eli was an earlier riser, used to arrive for work before dawn some days to count inventory and study the books. He was trying to pick up what he could about the business in the hopes of opening his own pharmacy one day. So if she was waiting on the steps like he said, then she'd headed here directly after I'd spoken with her in the kitchen.

"What did she want?" I asked.

I was there when Mr. Borden went through her bag this morning, every pocket, every seam of every dress. He'd found nothing, not so much as a wad of lint. That meant whatever she'd sought to purchase, she still had with her, hidden from me and her father.

"Prussic acid."

His whispered words carried with them an unsettling weight that left me gasping for breath. I recalled Mrs. Borden's hands trembling as she held that bottle, the one she said Mr. Borden had found hidden beneath the sack of pigeon feed in the barn.

"I didn't sell it to her," Eli quickly added as he reached out to steady my quivering hand. "I can't sell it without a prescription, and she didn't have one."

It took me a few long seconds to collect my thoughts, to steady my breath and still my mind enough to speak. "Did she argue?" I asked. "Did she get angry when you refused?"

"She did get angry. She claimed she'd bought it here before and they never questioned her about a prescription. But I know Mr. Smith; he would never allow anybody in his employment to sell prussic acid without a prescription." Eli's eyes trailed to the wooden file cabinet I could see in the back room. "I checked after she left," Eli continued. "Mr. Smith's records go back over ten years, Bridget, and I see to their organization myself every Friday eve. There is not one prescription in there for her. Never has been."

That didn't mean she hadn't bought it before. According to Mrs. Borden, she'd kept it hidden in the barn and used it on the last maid.

"What did she say she wanted it for?" I asked, quite sure it didn't matter. Whatever excuse Lizzie had fed him was most certainly a lie.

"A seal coat," Eli replied. "She said she needed it to clean a seal coat."

Eli adjusted the collar of his shirt, his face taking on that look again—the sad one that told me he'd seen through Lizzie straightaway this morning. Eli Bence knew exactly what I was dealing with, and rather than gossiping, he was quietly telling me. Warning me.

I got up from the seat with nothing more than a nod of appreciation in his direction. I knew why he was telling me this, knew that whatever gossip he'd heard about Lizzie Borden, had him fearing for my well-being. I also knew that Lizzie had no intention of cleaning a seal coat; she didn't even own one. I had a year's worth of seeing to her wardrobe to confirm that.

Chapter 32

I couldn't bring myself to worry about the thread or the mending waiting for me at home after talking with Eli Bence. I couldn't do much more than stand on Second Street and stare at the house as I listened to my heart pounding away in my chest.

It was mad. The whole thing was absolutely mad. No longer could I separate the Lizzie I *thought* I knew from the one who could have done this. There were too many things that didn't add up, too many moments when she was more of a stranger than a friend.

My mind drew in on itself as I thought about the previous maids. I wondered exactly how many had lived in that small attic space. How many poor, desperate women had attempted to navigate Lizzie and the darkness that constantly threatened to overtake her?

Setting my bag down on the small stoop outside the front door, I began digging for my keys. Before I'd even located them, I heard the locks shifting, the familiar sound of their metal sliding open.

"Bridget? What are you doing just standing out there?" Mrs. Borden pulled the door open, her eyes scanning the street behind me as she gestured me in.

"I was looking for my keys." I shifted in the doorway so I could see just beyond her into the darkened sitting room. "Is everything all right?"

"Yes. Of course. Come in."

She shut the door behind me, immediately setting about the arduous task of locking and double-checking each deadbolt. Her eyes darkened as she retreated into the sitting room. It was then that I saw him, Andrew Borden, sitting in the corner. His suit coat was wrinkled, his face drawn into a tight look of concern. My eyes widened as I took in the woman sitting next to him. Lizzie's best friend, Alice Russell. According to Lizzie, Alice hated Andrew Borden nearly as much as she. So why on earth was she here?

Mrs. Borden took my bag and pulled out the bottles, staring at their labels. "Why Smith's?" she asked. "We've instructed you to use Gallagher's."

"There was an incident there a short time back. With Lizzie. I thought it would be . . . ," I paused, trying hard to find the right word to explain my decision, "easier than dealing with Mr. Gallagher's stock boys."

She nodded as if she was aware of the incident. Of course she was. The whole town probably was.

Mr. Borden shifted in his chair, his gaze piercing and intense. "Lizzie has yet to come back today. Have you seen her?" His voice was hoarse, raspy as if he'd been shouting. Trouble with that theory, was that he hadn't, at least not that I'd heard. And with walls as paper thin as the ones in this house, I heard *everything*.

I took another quick scan of his face, noting the redness in his eyes and the shadows of exhaustion just beneath them. If I didn't know better, I'd think he'd been crying.

"No, sir. Not since this morning when I got up."

"And she didn't mention why she was home or where she was going at that time?" he shot back, his worry evident in the unusual slump of his frame. As a businessman, Mr. Borden prided himself on appearing confident. It was rare to see him like this—tired and unsure.

"No. She left without saying anything to me." I paused as Mrs. Borden slid the curtain open a crack and looked out. "She was headed for the barn. I'd presumed that she was still there when I left."

"She's not." He sighed, got up, and walked the few steps to where his wife stood. It was one of the few times I'd seen them this close; they looked like husband and wife as opposed to strangers housed under the same roof. He laid a hand on hers and nodded at Alice. "Lizzie's apparently in the midst of one of her fits again."

Alice's eyes met mine for a moment before flickering downward. Now that I got a closer look at her, I saw it—the exhaustion, the fear, the complete and utter confusion that came with being Lizzie's friend. I knew that look because I'd worn it myself, countless times.

"Lizzie came to me today," Alice whispered. "She was ranting, crazed. She said bad things were happening in this house. That she was afraid something was going to . . ."

I sucked in a breath of hot air, wishing the temperature in the room would drop enough for me to breathe easier. "Going to what?" I asked, confused as to why this, out of all of Lizzie's ramblings, would force Alice here, to speak directly with Mr. Borden himself. "And what kinds of bad things?"

My eyes darted between Alice and the Bordens. Mr. Borden just stood there stone-faced, as if Alice's fevered ramblings were nothing more than an annoyance. Mrs. Borden was trying hard to look unaffected, but I knew she was concerned. She kept straightening the front of her dress, her fingers grazing over the aging fabric repeatedly until it was smooth.

"That things were changing," Mrs. Borden mumbled under her breath.

Mr. Borden caught her whispered words and turned to her, his stoic mask cracking for a second as a flash of fury darkened his eyes. With nothing more than a blink, he shook it off and returned his attention to Alice. "Go on," he prompted.

"She was talking nonsense when she first arrived, was completely hysterical," Alice started, and I reached out my hand to steady her. She had begun swaying with her words, the color draining from her face as she replayed Lizzie's visit in her mind. "I wasn't sure what to say or what to do, so I just sat her down, gave her a glass of water, and waited until her nerves had calmed enough for her to talk with some sense."

Alice lifted her eyes from the rug, fixing her gaze on Mr. Borden. Tears stained her lashes, and her words came out in nothing more than a whispered hush. "Lizzie's never happy, surely you know that, sir."

"Lizzie's happiness is none of your concern, Alice," Mr. Borden replied.

Ignoring her husband's hand on her wrist, Mrs. Borden stepped forward, her voice going soft, pleading. "Tell us what she said, Alice."

I thought about Eli Bence's concerned expression and the way he'd taken me aside in the store. Either he was wrong . . . either everyone in this entire godforsaken town was mistaken about her, or Lizzie was truly going mad.

"She was going on about problems you were having with some of your tenants. She said that you had kicked them out because they were using your property for unseemly purposes. That she was—"

"My business dealing are not—"

I don't know whether Alice meant to cut him off or if she was so caught up in her own fear that she didn't hear his interrupted warning, because she continued without pause. "Lizzie said they broke into this house in broad daylight, while she and Emma and Mrs. Borden were home. That they were so angry with you that they went after her pigeons."

I stepped back at those words. Lizzie knew fair well who had slaughtered her pigeons, and it certainly wasn't an aggrieved tenant.

"She was rambling on about the house burning down around her, then she said she feared someone would hurt *you*, Mr. Borden."

"Did she say who?" Mr. Borden asked.

I searched his eyes for an inkling of fear, fear I wouldn't have blamed him for harboring. Instead, I saw determination . . . something akin to intent.

Alice shook her head and studied her shoes. "No, just that she feared your discourteous nature would bring you harm. Bring *her* harm."

Mr. Borden laughed, a full-blown chuckle that had us all backing away from him. "Nonsense," he said. "Simply Lizzie's paranoia influencing her thoughts again."

"I don't think so," Alice challenged. "She's prattled on before, but never like this. She was frightened, sir. Deathly so."

Mr. Borden took a step forward and motioned Alice to the door. "Thank you for your concern," he said formally. "I'll look into it. I'll have Mr. Morse ask around and see if there is any validity to her claims."

He opened the door and literally shooed her out. "And Alice," he called after her. "You did right coming to me. It's wise not to engage my daughter's delusions. And please, for your own safety, don't tell her we had this conversation."

Silenced by fear, Alice's hand froze on the latch to the gate. I don't know how long she stood there or when her composure broke. All I heard was the soft whimper of her tears as Mr. Borden slammed the door.

Chapter 33

I ran a fingertip over the worn headboard, every memory, every cramped and exhausting day I'd spent in this house rushing back to me. I hadn't expected it to all come to an end like this. But here I was, trying to keep my mind from veering off into the darkness while preparing to clean a house that held more secrets than the priest at St. Patrick's.

On top of Alice's words and the horrible, condemning thoughts that were swirling through my mind, I was sick. My stomach had been turning in on itself all day, and if I was right, Mrs. Borden was feeling ill too. Her face had been drawn into a tight knot last night after dinner, her hands repeatedly fluttering to her midsection as she swallowed back pain.

I thought about Eli's words and the prussic acid Lizzie had tried to purchase from him. About the bottle Mrs. Borden had locked away in the hutch in the parlor. About the unsettling calm hovering over this house.

After the incident with Alice, Mr. Borden forbade any of us from leaving. That had meant no fresh oyster soup, rather leftover mutton stew. Sure, I'd left the mutton stew unattended; it took hours to simmer, and I had chores to complete. But she wouldn't have . . . she couldn't have. Lizzie would never poison me.

A soft rap on my door drew my attention and I stood up, warily eyeing the handle. "Yes? Who's there?"

"John Morse." His voice was loud, booming, and I backed myself into the window, half-contemplated jumping out. "Let me in, Bridget. I know you're sick. Please."

It was the "please" that did me in, and I crossed the room, quietly unlocked my door, and opened it a crack. Mr. Morse was standing in the hallway, looking rumpled and tired. "Do you need something, sir?"

John pulled the hat from his head and ran a hand through his hair. "I need to speak with you. May I come in for a moment?"

I considered the question, every alarm in my body going off all at once. I'd never enjoyed being in the same room as Mr. Morse, thought it odd that he showed up whenever he pleased and with absolutely no rhyme or reason. He was friendly sometimes, cold and distant others, and I didn't have the strength or fortitude to guess which mood he was in now.

"I'm very busy, sir. If it's all the same to you, I'd rather be left alone."

"I doubt you are busy, Bridget. Truth be told, I believe you're hiding up here, and I don't blame you. Neither does Lizzie."

He was absolutely correct about what I was doing. I had a million chores to finish, yet I was hiding, praying that things would straighten themselves out without me.

"I'm not hiding," I spat out, frustrated with the fact that my own legs were quaking beneath me. "And what does Lizzie have to do with any of this?"

John exhaled loudly and leaned against my door frame. "Lizzie has everything to do with this, but I think you already know that."

I tossed the door open and flicked my hand in his direction. "Fine, then. Speak your mind."

An amused smile spread across his face as he stepped across my threshold and took in my room for the first time. "Listen, Bridget, I know what you must think of me. That I'm unsavory, popping in and out of here without any warning and making your job, your *life*, difficult."

I stared rather than answer. That was exactly how I felt.

"Do you know why I come here, though? Why I don't stay in Swansea and manage the affairs Andrew requests of me?"

"No, sir." *And I am not sure I care,* I silently said to myself.

John stood at a distance, as if he understood how uncomfortable I was with his presence in my room. It was more than awkward; it was utterly inappropriate.

"I'm not here to offend your sensibilities. I do help keep an eye on the farm and mediate things with the tenants. But I also see what is happening here . . . the problems in this house and Lizzie's erratic behavior."

John's forehead crumpled, his entire demeanor shifting into one of frustration and disappointment. "I've been visiting with my nieces for years, and I've seen plenty more than you will ever know. I was here the day each of them was born, and made a promise to my sister Sarah that I would look after them, see that they didn't fall into their father's dreary ways. I have failed my sister, failed Lizzie and Emma, and, in a way, you."

"I don't follow," I said, quite certain I didn't like the direction this conversation was headed.

"Andrew and Abigail have enough money to buy half of the houses on the Hill, you know that, right?"

I nodded, but stayed silent. While I wasn't privy to exactly how much money Mr. Borden had accrued, I knew it was significant. I often wondered why they lived on Second Street when most people of their station lived on the Hill.

"When Lizzie falls ill with one of her fits, she wanders. Says strange things. Believes strange things. It's much easier to control a situation like that here, where the only folks who might see her are street peddlers."

Situation. Like everyone else, it was becoming abundantly clear that John Morse believed Lizzie to be a problem and nothing more. She was a liability to be watched over, a woman with a large mouth and sticky hands, just as Liam believed. No wonder she was so bitter, why she constantly fought her parents. They'd created a mold for her no one should have to fit into.

"She's not a *situation*, Mr. Morse. She's confused, sad . . . a lot of things. I see it. Even her friend Alice sees it. But nothing ever seems to change; no one in this house ever finds any peace."

"Abigail cares, more than you will ever know. And you are right. I am sorry; I should not have referred to Lizzie so callously. What I meant to say was that Lizzie needs help; more help than you can give her. I'm not saying it's her fault or that there's anyone to blame here. She's a victim of circumstance, so far as I can tell."

"What circumstance?"

"It was insane, really. One minute my sister was alive, well, and full of life. She was looking forward to having more children, giving Andrew a son. Then the next thing I know, she's . . . " Mr. Morse trailed off, his eyes fluttering closed as if he was lost in a distant memory. "She was just gone. No one could really explain it, not even the doctors. The whole house changed that day. Andrew changed that day."

There was a long pause, one I wasn't sure how I was supposed to respond to. I thought if I stayed silent and looked anywhere but at him, that I could ignore the desperation and sadness I could hear in his voice. But I couldn't; it seeped into me like every other toxin in this house.

"It must be hard for you." John started speaking again, his voice dipping to a barely audible level. "I understand why you are leaving. In fact, I think it is the change she needs to finally set things in motion."

"She?" I whispered.

Mr. Morse shook his head rather than answer. "Lizzie and Andrew have been locked in this battle for years. It's raged around me, around Abigail, and now it's raging around you."

I inched back. His agitated tone unnerved me. In all his countless visits, as I made his eggs, folded his sheets, and laundered his clothes, Mr. Morse had never spoken to me this way. He'd always been calm and collected.

Mr. Morse lifted his hands into the air. "I can see that I've alarmed you, and I'm sorry for that. That was never my intention. Ever. I just wanted you to know that I feel it too. The darkness in this house."

He leaned over and gently placed his hand on my shoulder. "Don't let it suck you in, Bridget. Don't let the voices that the rest of them hear transfer to you."

His words echoed through my mind, the honesty of them settling around me like a heavy cloak. If John Morse could feel it, if a man who had nothing to gain from telling me any of this sensed it, then it had to be real.

Chapter 34

I nearly doubled over as I pulled my body out of bed, forcing my eyes to begin the task of focusing again. My stomach spasmed in pain and I was exhausted, so tired I could barely think.

I'd heard Lizzie arguing with her father just yesterday about fetching Dr. Bowen from across the street. Mrs. Borden seemed to be suffering the most. With her chamber pot full, she'd barely made it to the cellar privy last night, never mind the outhouse. But Mr. Borden wouldn't hear of fetching the doctor; he said the cost was burdensome and wholly unnecessary for what amounted to nothing more than a sour stomach. Listening to Mrs. Borden retch these past two nights, I would've gladly paid the cost myself, if I'd had it.

I'd crawled into bed over an hour ago, consumed with nausea and the heat of the day. I'd washed every window on the main floor this morning, and between the sun beating down and the thickness of the air settling into my lungs, I'd needed a break. A short nap. Something to take the edge off my exhaustion. Besides that, I craved an escape. A few minutes away from Mrs. Borden's heartbroken gaze and depressed shuffling. From Andrew Borden's solemn expressions and Lizzie's temper. From Mr. Morse's dark honesty. I was close to my breaking point. So close.

I'd fallen asleep to the taste of rancid mutton stew rising in my throat, and tossed and turned as I dreamed about a sealskin coat

Lizzie didn't own. I walked down the front staircase in my dream and drew open the hutch to see the bottle of prussic acid missing. I felt the blood of the pigeons coating my hands, smelled their meaty flesh simmering in the pot. It all came to a horrific end as Liam's face twisted into that of Mr. Borden's. The brightness of his eyes and the promise of a future . . . our future, died out as I floated through the rooms of this darkened house.

I came awake with a start, a muffled scream barely escaping my lips. The haze of sleep quickly lifted, and I wondered if I was next in the long line of maids Lizzie had pushed away, threatened, or poisoned until they crawled from this house defeated and seeking the safety of the streets.

But I wasn't like the other maids. I refused to believe that the hours Lizzie and I had spent talking each day, the way she would help me with the most menial of chores and lie to her father to protect me, meant nothing. I refused to believe she'd intentionally hurt me, never mind poison me. She was my friend, same as Minnie. Same as Seamus. At the very least, I owed her the opportunity to explain, to hear from Lizzie's own mouth what she was up to. If I didn't, I'd be no better than the shopkeepers and townswomen who gossiped behind her back every day. I was her friend, and friends owed each other that much.

I cracked open my bedroom door and listened for any indication that Mr. Borden had come home or that John Morse was wandering about again.

Muttering a curse under my breath, I loosened the ties of my apron as I made my way down the stairwell. They were digging into me, the scratchy cloth adhering to my sweat-soaked skin. This was the hottest month I could recall in years. Everyone else in Fall River was taking up spots near the river to cool down, but not us. No. We were stuck here, trapped on Second Street, simmering in our own illness.

It was dark in the hallway, but that was to be expected. With no windows nearby, it was impossible to get any natural light or any fresh air into that cramped space. The smell of rotting meat and chamber pots filled the air, and I gagged, nearly tossed the contents of my stomach right there on the back wall.

I rounded the second-floor landing and noticed the door to Mr. Borden's room was ajar. I'd check with Mrs. Borden. Perhaps she had purposely left it unlocked so she didn't have to fumble with the knob as she raced for the cellar privy. She was the only one in the house with me as far as I knew. Lizzie was in the barn searching for her iron sinkers, and Mr. Borden was attending to his morning affairs. When I'd spoken with Mrs. Borden a short hour ago, she was changing the sheets and airing out the guest room. Much to everyone's relief, Mr. Morse hadn't fallen ill. She was planning on moving him out of the attic room into the guest room in the hopes of keeping him healthy. Not that I had complained. But moving him downstairs would hopefully afford my mind a bit more rest.

I nudged the door open the rest of the way and peered into the room. The door connecting the Bordens' bedroom to Mr. Borden's upstairs study was open a sliver, the slightest beam of flickering light casting a shadow into the hallway. Initially, I thought this was Lizzie's doing. She'd been quiet, unsettlingly so, since returning, and this would be just the kind of childish behavior—unlocking her father's study door—she would do to set him on edge.

I kept my footsteps light as I edged towards the door, listening. Surrounded by nothing but the sound of my own breathing, I pushed the door wide and walked in, curious to see what Lizzie had taken this time.

She'd done it before, stolen stuff right out of his room and then blamed it on nonexistent prowlers. The first time it had been nothing more than some streetcar tickets, change, and Mr. Borden's pocket watch, but it was enough to send him into a fit of paranoia. He'd called the police, even went so far as to insinuate that it was one of his disgruntled tenants, but the police didn't put much effort into locating the thief.

It was I who'd found the watch. It had been tucked behind the ash bin in the cellar. I searched for a bit that day but never found the other things; I'd assumed Lizzie had spent the money or donated it to one of her charities.

I'd only been in this room a handful of times. Mr. Borden insisted that his wife maintain their personal space, only allowing me to help with the heavy spring and fall cleaning. But I didn't need to have intimate knowledge of his room to know something was amiss. The bed was disheveled, the doors to the wardrobe swung open, and Mrs. Borden's dress was shoved hastily inside an open trunk on the bed.

Scattered around the trunk were papers and a small satchel I'd seen Mrs. Borden use to carry her money. I sifted through them, my eyes settling on the pocket watch I'd seen hidden in the cellar, the one I'd assumed Lizzie had stolen.

I pushed the watch aside, my attention drifting to the two documents sitting beneath it—the deed to the house on Ferry Street, the same one Lizzie and Emma had sold back to their father earlier this summer, and two tickets for the Old Colony & Fall River Railroad to Boston.

Two tickets . . . both dated today. The three o'clock train, to be exact. Yet the open trunk appeared to contain only Abigail's clothes; Mr. Borden's were still hanging neatly in the wardrobe.

No wonder she kept telling me everything was going to be all right eventually. She wasn't just getting me out of this house, she was planning on leaving as well.

I took a quick peek at Mr. Borden's desk. The key to this room, the one he left on the mantel to taunt Lizzie, was sitting next to yesterday's mail. None of his papers looked out of order; they were neatly stacked, his ink blotter anchoring them in place. I pulled at the handle to the safe. It was still locked, didn't give an inch.

A shadow passed over the entrance to Lizzie's room, and I walked in that direction, surprised to see the door connecting her room to that of her parents unlocked and standing open. A thick and heavy smell permeated the air. It reminded me of the smoke that billowed out from the iron works, combined with the scent of the outhouse on a hot summer day.

Covering my nose so as not to further upset my already delicate stomach, I slipped into Lizzie's empty room. The odor was stronger in here, and I did a quick circle to find its source. This room was as silent as the last, the curtains drawn tight across the sole window. I drew back the lace covering the window, fully intent on airing out Lizzie's room. There was no way she'd be able to breathe tonight with that putrid stench surrounding her.

Light drifted into the room, bouncing off the few bottles of powder and perfume Lizzie had on her dressing table. One in particular caught my attention, the rays of the sun filtering through the clear liquid, casting a rainbow of colors across a fur coat draped across her bed.

I would've thought it odd that Lizzie was dawdling with a fur coat in the heat of the summer, had I not talked to Eli. Had I not instinctively gathered what it was. A seal coat.

It was gray, with tiny flecks of white marking the fur. I ran my hand across the soft fur, slipping it into one of its pockets. My fingers curled around a piece of paper and I pulled it out, angling it towards the light of the window so I could make out the words. It was a receipt dated three days earlier, from a clothier's in New Bedford.

I shoved my hand into the other pocket and came up with a clear bottle. Cursing myself for continually distrusting Lizzie, I brought the bottle to my nose, wondering if it was the source of the stench that had befallen the house. I smiled as I inhaled the sweet scent. It was nothing more than the jasmine oil Lizzie had taken to wearing on occasion.

Here I was, convinced that Lizzie was starting trouble, ready to flee this house out of fear she was trying to poison me along with her own parents, and all along she was in fact telling the truth.

Swiping at my eyes, I stood up and grabbed the coat. I tucked the receipt and the bottle of perfume back into the pocket, then hung it in her wardrobe closet. I'd ask her about it later, apologize for ever distrusting her, and then inform Mrs. Borden and Liam that I wasn't leaving, that I was staying right here with my friend. With Lizzie.

Chapter 35

I made my way back through Mr. Borden's room and locked his door with the key I'd found sitting on his desk. I dropped the key into the pocket of my apron and headed through Lizzie's room for the front staircase, intent on locking the main door to his and Mrs. Borden's bedroom as well. No doubt he'd know someone had been in his room—he had an uncanny ability to know when his personal space had been disturbed. I just hoped he wouldn't suspect Lizzie or me.

I jammed the key in the lock, the sound of its sliding into place echoing through the house like thunder. I turned around and made my way back to the front staircase. My eyes paused at the entrance to the guest room . . . to the quarters John Morse would be using this evening.

I could see her feet, the soles of her shoes sticking out from the side of the bed. It was almost as if she'd gone to sleep and fallen out of the bed, her body lying there motionless. Swallowing back the sensation of dread, I took a step in her direction and whispered her name. "Mrs. Borden?"

Silence settled around the heavy air and I inched into the room. I stopped cold and listened for the slightest sound—a pained intake of breath, a twitch of a muscle . . . anything to contradict what I was seeing.

There were flecks of red coating the carpet by her feet, and even more on the wall above her head. I put one knee onto the bed and peered over the other side. There was a pool of red where her head lay, her eyes . . . her entire face turned in the opposite direction.

"Mrs. Borden," I choked out again as I hurried to the far side of the bed. I knew I should've insisted on changing the sheets myself. She'd looked so drawn and tired when I spoke with her earlier today. No doubt she'd lain down for a spot of rest, had woken disorientated, and had fallen from the bed. It wouldn't surprise me, not given how sick she'd been. I just hoped that I wasn't too late.

I skidded to a stop at the end of the bed, my eyes wide as I took in the unimaginable. Abigail Borden's body lay face down, a deep river of blood oozing from the back of her skull and out onto the floral rug. Her arms were bent up beneath her thick frame, and she was still. Completely still.

I put my hand on her back, flinching at the cold radiating from beneath her blouse. Her hair . . . no, her entire braid was on the floor next to her, scalped from her head. Deep lacerations crisscrossed the back of her skull. Entire pieces of bone were missing, and sharp bits of white jutted out from the leathery gray of her brain.

I quickly scanned the room, searching for whatever . . . whoever had done this. I saw nothing. No bloody footprints, no weapons, no predator hiding in the corner. Nothing but complete orderliness, marred by Mrs. Borden's brutalized body.

A muted thump sounded downstairs, and I forced myself to breathe deep as the icy grip of terror began to take hold. Someone was in the house. Whoever had done this was still in the house.

I eased back out the door, desperately trying to keep my footsteps light. I had a clear view of the front door from the top of the landing. It was closed up tight, the lock engaged, the entryway silent.

I dug the key out of my apron pocket and jammed it into the door that connected Lizzie's room to her parents'. The lock there was nothing more than a spring latch, and would be easier and quicker to manipulate than the front.

I cleared the first few steps, my attention focused solely on getting outside as quickly as my feet could carry me, when I ran smack into her. I would've toppled down the stairs had she not placed a steadying hand on my shoulder.

"Bridget?" Lizzie asked, her hands holding my trembling body still. "What is it? What's wrong?"

Quickly, I scanned her dress. Same plain blue dress she'd had on this morning at breakfast, and with the exception of a spot of dirt from rummaging through the barn, it was completely clean. No blood, no hair, not even a pleat out of place.

"Bridget?" She shook me hard this time, forcing me to meet her eyes. "What is going on?"

I grabbed her hand, and rather than answer, dragged her up the steps and into her father's room. If she was surprised to find it unlocked, she didn't let on. She followed me in and stared at the open chest and train tickets on the bed.

"What is—" Lizzie went to sift through the open trunk, and I yanked her hand hard. We didn't have time to sort through her stepmother's things. I needed her to see what had happened, to see firsthand that her stepmother was dead, slaughtered in her own house. Then we needed to get out of here and get to Liam's, where he and Seamus could keep us safe.

I stopped at the door to the guest room. I wasn't going back in there. I was certain the image of Mrs. Borden's butchered body would haunt my every dream for years to come. I didn't need another look to nourish my nightmares.

"Look," I whispered as I gently nudged Lizzie into the room. "Just look at what they did to her."

"To who?" Lizzie asked, not moving.

"Your stepmother. Abigail. She's gone. Dead."

Lizzie shook me off, stifling a laugh. "Don't be silly, Bridget. I am sure she is just sleeping off whatever illness has plagued this house. If Father had just let Dr. Bowen see to her yesterday like she asked, then—"

"No, she won't be fine," I said, cutting her off. "She's not sick; she's dead. Her hair. It's hacked off. Her head . . . it's . . . it's . . ."

I couldn't get the words out, couldn't even begin to describe the sight of her broken skull. Fragments missing, shards of bone mingled with the blood pooling on the rug. Her scalp ripped clean from her brain. She hadn't simply been killed, she'd been hacked to death.

Something in my hurried words made Lizzie take notice. She gently eased me back against the banister, her hand resting on my shoulder in silent reassurance. "Stay here," she said. "Don't go anywhere or do anything without me."

I closed my eyes and counted her footsteps, knew the instant she came upon Mrs. Borden's body. Lizzie's gasp echoed off the walls, and I could almost hear the silent scream tearing from her chest.

"What happened?" She was standing in front of me now, the words tumbling from her lips in a rushed demand. "Bridget. What. Happened?"

"I don't know," I choked out. My eyes refused to leave the red stains on her palms. Like in a bad dream, that red seemed to grow until it swallowed everything in my line of vision. I shook my head, desperate to keep my grip on my sanity.

"Did you do this?"

Lizzie's voice broke through the haze of red, and I stepped back. There wasn't an ounce of anger in her tone, no reproach, not even a tinge of fear. If anything, there was an unspoken promise there, one that said she'd protect me, keep me safe regardless of my answer.

"God, no. You have to believe me. I didn't do this. I could never." My voice rose in panic. Of course she thought I did it, anyone would. I was the only one home . . . a poor Irish maid who in a few weeks would no longer be employed by the Bordens. No one would ask why; they'd assume I'd been dismissed. That I was angry. Vengeful.

"He's going to think I did it. Your father. Mr. Morse . . . they are all going to believe it was me." I'd seen it happen before; a poor Irish immigrant thrown in jail for something he didn't do because a person of wealth pointed a finger in his direction. I was no different, and Mr. Borden certainly carried influence in Fall River.

The expression that came over her face was gentle and short-lived, overshadowed by the fear that whoever had done this was possibly still in the house, waiting for us. Waiting for her. "No one is going to blame you, Bridget, ever. I give you my word."

Chapter 36

The entire house seemed to hum with a dark energy. A wordless, soundless evil that swept up through the staircase and settled into every corner. It was a sinister calm, one that had me searching every second of the past week, trying to figure out who would do this, and why.

I was frozen in place, my feet melded to the top of the landing as my mind churned. I needed to get out of this house. I needed to run to Liam and never look back. Yet I couldn't even muster the courage to speak, never mind move.

"Bridget?"

My eyes were fixed on the front window of the house as I quickly tried to calculate the distance to the street below. It was the quickest way out. Maybe the only way out.

"Bridget." There it was again, my name floating through the air, pulling at me to respond. I quickly turned my head towards Lizzie's room. If I could make my way to the back of the house, then maybe I could use the back staircase, hide out in the cellar behind the ash bin until nightfall, then slip out unnoticed.

I didn't see her raise her hand, but seconds later I felt the impact, the stinging burn blooming across my cheek. She'd hit me. Lizzie had actually hit me.

Whatever had me trapped in my mind was gone, replaced with raw anger. And burning pain. I reached up to cradle my face, stunned.

"Good," she said before I could react. "I need you to keep your wits about you, Bridget. Now, I asked you a question. Is anyone else in the house?"

I shook my head. I remembered John Morse and Mr. Borden talking after breakfast. If their raised voices were any indication, tensions had been high between them. But they'd both left shortly thereafter, Mr. Borden to attend to his morning duties and John Morse . . . well, I didn't know where he was off to. I hadn't cared before now.

"Just me and Mrs. Borden," I said. "I was washing windows, then laid down when the heat got the best of me. Your stepmother said she was going to change the linens and air out the guest room so Mr. Morse could retire there this evening."

Lizzie shook her head, a look of confusion crossing her features. "That doesn't make any sense. Uncle John is leaving this afternoon. He told me so this morning. Abigail was there as well; she heard him clear as me."

"So that's who the other ticket is for," I said.

"What other ticket? What are you going on about?"

"The tickets on your father's bed. There were two of them. Both leaving today," I said, acknowledging a fact I hadn't quite wrapped my own mind around. "Mrs. Borden's clothes were packed, but your father's—"

"Bridget, stop," Lizzie said to me. "It doesn't matter what you saw or what you think you saw. We need to leave now and alert the police. Where Abigail was going and with whom isn't important. Not when whoever did this could still be in the house."

I looked down at the splatters of blood coating the floral rug, then at my hands. They were shaking, trembling violently as I clutched at the folds of my skirts. I wasn't an idiot. I knew what people would think, knew that for a brief second, Lizzie had assumed the worst of me herself.

"If they lock me away, promise me you will take care of my sister," I pleaded.

Lizzie grabbed my hand and yanked me towards the front stairwell. "I won't need to take care of your sister. I'm going to tell everyone I was home too, that you were with me in the barn looking for the sinkers when it happened."

I grabbed onto doorknob and refused to let go. "Promise me, Lizzie. It's my fault Cara is the way she is, and I need to know she'll be looked after."

She nodded once. "Like you, I consider her one of my own and would take care of her as such. I've never lied to you, Bridget, not once. And I'm not lying now when I say that when I'm through with this town, nobody will cast suspicion your way. *Nobody.*"

Chapter 37

Each of the thirteen steps creaked under our weight and we paused on each one, half-expecting to be caught and hacked to death ourselves. The front door came into view, and I nearly cried out in relief. We were close, so close to getting out.

My eyes traveled the length of the deadbolts, wondering how we were possibly going to get them unlocked without calling attention to ourselves. On days like today, when the humidity swelled them tight, they were loud, often stuck. And right now, my hands were neither steady nor firm.

I was furiously trying to the twist the deadbolt open when Lizzie laid a silencing hand on my shoulder and motioned to the small table in the entryway. There was a package sitting there, and next to it was Mr. Borden's ring of keys. I immediately understood her unspoken plea. Her father was home, and regardless of the strife between them, he needed to be warned.

"Did you see him when you came in?" I asked, hoping we didn't have to wander through every one of the downstairs rooms looking for him.

She shook her head, and I took a steadying breath. Andrew Borden may have been a miserable old man who cherished his holdings more than his family, but he was Lizzie's father, and I wouldn't leave the dangerous task of warning him to Lizzie alone.

We slowly inched our way into the sitting room and saw him standing by the unlit fireplace. He was staring at the mantel, his shoulders hunched forward and his back to us. He hadn't heard us enter, but we had kept our footsteps purposely light for fear of the murderer.

"Father," Lizzie whispered.

He didn't respond, no hitch in his breathing, not even a nod of his head to indicate he realized we were there. It was as if his mind was impervious to anything around him, his eyes completely focused on that tiny spot on the mantel.

I took a step forward, wondering what had Mr. Borden so entranced, but Lizzie swept her hand out to the side, stopping me. "Father," she whispered again, her hand coming to rest on his upper arm. "We need to leave. Now."

I thought it odd that Lizzie didn't tell him why. Perhaps she didn't want to agitate him, risk causing a scene that would draw the perpetrator's attention before we were all safely outside. Or perhaps she knew more than she was letting on and was approaching him as if he were a skittish foal for a reason . . . a dark, deadly reason.

Mr. Borden flinched at the contact, a violent tremor working its way through his body. He raised his head as if to speak, but nothing came out. I waited for his words, counting the seconds in time with the clock. Seconds turned into minutes and all we got from him was silence. Terrifying silence.

"Father?" Lizzie repeated. She stepped around him, hoping to catch his attention and break him from whatever thought had him trapped in immobility.

Her face went pale, every ounce of color draining from her cheeks as she reached for me. She swatted me backwards, sweeping her hand out in the direction of the door. "Bridget, go. Now."

I widened my stance and stood firm. I wasn't leaving her here. I wasn't leaving Mr. Borden here. "Mr. Borden, please mind Lizzie's

words. We have to leave this house and fetch the police. Your wife
. . . Mrs. Borden . . . something has happened to her."

Mr. Borden turned at the sound of my voice, his movements
slow, drawn out, as if dealing with my interference was costing
him more energy than he wished to expend. "I am well aware of
what has befallen my precious wife. Do you think me ignorant of
what goes on in my own home?"

I drew a hand up to cover my mouth as he turned and took a
step towards me. The black suit coat he wore each day was perfectly
pressed in the back, not a stitch of lint or a pulled seam. But
the front . . . the front was stained. Splatters of crimson covered
him from his neck to his ankles. Long strands of brown hair had
dried onto his white shirt and a few remained tangled between
his fingers. His face was flushed, his wrinkles etched with what I
could only assume was blood. And that dull look in his eyes was
back, the same dead expression I'd seen on him when he killed the
pigeons.

The sound that tore from my throat was feral, something
between a cry and a screech. I covered my ears and squeezed my
eyes shut in a futile attempt to drown it all out. He was there in
a second, his bloodied hand clamping down over my mouth, the
taste of blood . . . of Abigail Borden's blood making me gag.

"Scream and you will suffer her fate," he warned, as he let go
and took a tentative step back. "The police will be notified in due
time, my dear. All in due time."

I followed Lizzie's gaze to the corner of the room, gasping at the
axe propped against the wall. Everything, including the handle,
was coated in blood. That was the last thing Abigail Borden had
known before she died—the biting edge of that blade and the
crazed look of rage in her husband's eyes.

"Why?" Lizzie choked out.

I grasped Lizzie's arm and yanked hard. *Why* didn't matter.
I didn't care why Mr. Borden had killed his wife or if he even

remembered. All that mattered was getting out of there before he turned on me and Lizzie.

Lizzie pushed me away. She was bigger than me, stronger, and it took virtually all of my effort to stay upright. "What have you done?" Lizzie asked again. Her voice was calm, collected, as if the question she was posing were no different than one about where he'd laid the mail. It was peculiar, and it had my head shifting between her and her father, trying to gauge who was crazier.

"There's nothing worse than a liar . . . a fraud," he growled, his jaw clenching and unclenching beneath his blood-crusted beard. "And there is nothing I value more than loyalty and family. She destroyed both. She's been planning it for years. Taking money and valuables. Hiding them in this house and plotting with *him*."

His gaze softened as he turned to Lizzie, his voice dropping in remorse. "All the while I thought it was you who was stealing from this family. She led me to believe it was you. My own daughter. My own blood."

Chapter 38

I watched the edges of Andrew Borden's mouth turn up into a cruel smile. "You can't think I was going to simply allow her to leave. Stand by and do nothing as she made a mockery of me, of this family?" He was drawing closer to Lizzie now, daring her to do anything but listen.

"You know, I did Abigail a favor by marrying her. She was nothing more than a spinster without a single prospect. No money to even keep a proper home. I gave her my name and a place in society, and this is how she repays me. This."

Lizzie shook her head. "You're mad!" She whirled in my direction, would've knocked me down if Andrew hadn't grabbed her by the arm and yanked her back.

"Am I?" Mr. Borden chuckled. "Actually, it's *you* the entire town believes to be prone to fits. No one will suspect me of this, Lizzie. If anything, they'll suspect *her*," Andrew said, his head snapping in my direction, "A poor Irish maid who'd been relieved of her duties, one who has already tried to poison us, and who my wife suspects is taking up with John Morse."

His eyes shifted from Lizzie to me, a twisted smile of acknowledgment spreading across his face. "That is what the letter says, is it not? That you were dismissed from my house because of your unseemly behavior, taking up with my brother-in-law right under this roof."

Lizzie's eyes met mine. There was a silent question there, one the simultaneously broke my heart and had me seething mad. "That's not true. She made that up; she said it was Mr. Morse who had shown interest in me. She was helping me find new employment, 'tis all. It was a lie . . . a story she made up so no one would ask questions."

"See," he said, turning his eyes back to Lizzie. "That dear stepmother of yours was forcing her away too, stripping you of the one friend you had. Now you see why I did it, why this family is better off with her gone?"

"I'll tell them the truth." The words tumbled from my mouth before I could stop them. "I'll tell everybody who will listen what I saw in this house, what you did to Lizzie's pigeons. What you did to Mrs. Borden."

I caught a glimpse of Lizzie's fearful face from the corner of my eye and nodded. I didn't care if I was tempting a madman. I was done living in darkness, done pretending I didn't see or hear what went on in this house. I'd back up every rumor I ever heard about this family because at the end of the day, they weren't rumors . . . they were the sordid truth. Mr. Borden was a miserly man who stifled his daughter's wit and spoke of her as if she was touched in the head. Sure Lizzie may have stolen a corset and kept pigeons as pets, but it was Andrew Borden, not Lizzie, who carried the Borden curse.

"I know the truth, and I'll be damned if I'm going to watch you lie about it," I said through clenched teeth.

Mr. Borden returned his focus to me and I froze, my boots melded to the floor beneath me as my eyes darted in every direction, looking for an escape. He grabbed me, and I nearly toppled over onto the couch as I tried to wrench myself from his grasp.

I closed my eyes and waited for my world to end. I'd seen what Andrew Borden was capable of the day he dropped the pigeons onto the table, seen it lying upstairs in a puddle of blood and bone shards on the bedroom floor. The demons had gotten into his soul, burrowed in so deep that all hope was gone.

Lizzie was yelling in the background, her voice barely audible through the ringing in my ears. I tried to hone in on that sound, the high pitch of her anger. I found it, was turning my head in her direction, when the entire room went silent. Deadly silent.

My name floated through the thick air, the sweet sound of Liam's voice breaking through the vicious white noise. But he sounded angry, enraged, and much too close. I pried my eyes open, the edges of my vision growing hazy as I blinked back tears. I saw the wooden axe handle, stared at it in horror as it struck the back of Mr. Borden's head. His entire face bloomed with anger, then went slack.

He fell, his body slumping sideways onto the couch, pulling me down with him. My feet slid against the floor as I tried desperately to find purchase. I gasped as a thick stream of blood began flowing down the right side of Mr. Borden's head, coating his gray hair with red. I stayed still, half-lying under Mr. Borden's unconscious form, watching, waiting for him to move.

It wasn't the muted thump of the axe hitting the floor that brought me back to my senses, rather a strong set of arms pulling me to my feet and the sweet scent of sweat and stale beer that I'd come to love. That I'd come to associate with only one person. Liam.

"Are you all right, love?" Liam asked as he turned me in his arms, his fingers whispering over my face as if looking for some injury. "Did he hurt you?"

Trembling, I looked up at him, completely incapable of responding. I wasn't all right. This house . . . this family was far from all right.

"Abi—" My words were choked off by movement on the couch. Mr. Borden was coming around, mumbling incoherently as he struggled to get his bearings. It wasn't the axe handle Seamus used this time to knock him out, but his fist. It slammed into Mr. Borden's face, his head snapping back before he rolled over onto his side.

A tiny bottle slipped from his pocket, teetering on the edge of the couch before falling to the floor. I waited for it to crack, to splinter into a thousand pieces. It didn't. It simply settled there by his feet, the name of the poisonous acid etched into the clear glass, staring up at me.

Lizzie shoved Seamus out of the way, all but knocked him over in her attempt to retrieve the bottle. She picked it up and uncorked it, holding it up to her nose as if to confirm what she already knew.

"Prussic acid," she whispered.

She held the bottle up for me to see, but I didn't need an explanation or even visual proof of what Mr. Borden had been planning. It wasn't Lizzie who had tampered with the mutton stew. It wasn't she who had caused the previous maid's sudden departure. It was Mr. Borden.

I leaned over and retched, nothing but dry air heaving from my stomach. He'd made us sick—Abigail, Lizzie, even me—and then refused to call the doctor, claimed he saw no need to part with a single dime over something that would pass in a day or two.

"He's the reason Mrs. Borden was sick. He's the reason we are all sick. And when we didn't die fast enough, when his wife got better, he . . . he . . . "

Liam leaned down so his eyes were inches from mine, as he took my head in his hands and willed me to calm down and tell him what had happened. I couldn't. The fear, the guilt for questioning Lizzie, the anger . . . it was all too unfathomable.

"She's upstairs . . . the axe . . . hacked. Hair . . . all gone." The words sputtered from my mouth as if I were a child. Despite Liam's grip on me, my body sank to the floor as I prayed for the blackness dancing in my vision to take me, to pull me under, to where I didn't have to think. Where I didn't have to smell the rotten stench of mutton stew and vomit, or see Mrs. Borden's dead eyes staring back at me.

"Seamus, go." It was two short words, but Seamus understood what his brother meant. If neither Lizzie nor I had the presence of mind to speak, then he'd go see for himself.

Seamus's heavy treads stopped abruptly at the top of the stairs, the sudden thud against the wall telling me he needed the dark wall of this cursed house to hold him up as he took in Mrs. Borden's body.

I didn't recall him coming back down the stairs or what he said. I just remembered him walking past me, past his brother until he stood dead center in front of Lizzie.

"Did you do that?" he asked her.

Lizzie's eyes flicked towards Seamus, clouded and as dark as the coal used to heat the house. She didn't respond, didn't even acknowledge his presence, just gently placed the bottle of prussic acid into her pocket and skirted around him.

"I asked you a question, lass," Seamus hollered as he latched onto her wrist. "And I expect an answer."

Lizzie lowered her eyes, her attention fully focused on the fingers Seamus had banded around her wrist. "Take your hand off me." There was no hitch in her voice, not the slightest hint of anger or fear. Just that same, eerily calm determination I'd heard moments ago from her father.

Seamus's hand flexed tighter, Lizzie's fingers going white under the pressure. Without so much as a second warning, she latched onto him and dug her nails in, scoring their sharp edges down the back of his hand until he jolted back in pain and let her go.

"You asked me if I killed my own stepmother," Lizzie said as she picked up the axe. "You expect an answer, boy? Well, here it is."

It took only a second for Lizzie to adjust her grip, to spread her hands further apart on the handle and widen her stance. Liam shoved me hard behind him, my back connecting with the corner of the mantel. Seamus joined him, his hand sweeping out, cornering me behind their bodies.

I caught the glint of the blade as she swung it through the air and I clearly recall the sound of it melding with her father's skull, the dull crack of the bone, and the way his head clung to the axe as she tugged it free. I remember it all, every crushing blow, every drop of blood coating the wall.

Chapter 39

"No, I did not kill Abigail," Lizzie hissed as she raised the axe above her head and swung it down again. It caught the side of Mr. Borden's face this time, leaving his flesh hanging from a massive, jagged hole. The axe slid free from his head with ease, and she swung it again and again, each hit punctuated by a declaration . . . each born of thirty-two years of pain and repressed fury.

"I would never kill Abigail, and I would never poison Bridget." Her last declaration came with the fiercest of blows, her strength shattering her father's skull, splitting his left eye socket in half and taking his nose.

Every injustice Mr. Borden had ever served his daughter came out that day. The pigeons. The corsets. The house on Ferry Street. Every maid she had befriended, whom he'd purposefully scared away. Every horrible lie he'd ever told to make her seem weak and unworthy in society's eyes. The death of her mother and the alienation of Emma. All of her anger, every last bit of vengeance, was set free in the eleven blows she delivered to her father's head.

None of us stopped her. Part of it was our own fear, and part of it was awe. Mostly, we didn't stop her because what she was saying as she struck her blows, the dirty secrets she was spewing forth, had earned Mr. Borden this fate. If what Lizzie was saying was true—and I'd wager my life that it was—then neither me, nor Liam, nor Seamus saw fit to show this vile man mercy.

Lizzie caught the top of his skull with the last blow, the axe so deeply embedded that it refused to let go. She yanked back hard, nearly lost her footing as her feet slipped in the blood collecting on the floor. Not in her right mind and determined to strike again, she anchored her feet against the legs of the couch and pulled with all her might. The handle splintered, small shards of wood raining down before it broke off entirely.

Lizzie fell backwards, the handle still melded to her hands, the head of the axe still wedged in Mr. Borden's skull. In a second, she was back on her feet, her hands outstretched towards the heavy piece of flint.

Seamus tackled her, his body rolling to the floor with her. She screamed as she struck at his face over and over again, leaving behind ribbons of pink. He refused to let her go, just pulled her back into his chest and wrapped his feet around her waist, holding her there until her body and mind gave in to exhaustion.

"Shh, lass, it's all right," he soothed, whispering to her in the same gentle tone I'd heard him take countless times with Minnie, when the ale wreaked havoc on her senses and her stomach. "You can stop now. He's gone; he can't hurt you anymore."

Never once had I seen Lizzie cry. Not when her own father slaughtered her pigeons. Not over the insidious gossip that seemed to plague her. Not when she talked about the mother she'd lost or when Emma made it her purpose to escape Fall River as often as possible, leaving Lizzie alone to suffer. Now her tears ran freely, streaming down her face, mingling with the blood that coated both her hands and Seamus's.

It wasn't until her body stilled that Liam let me out from behind his sheltering stance. I slid to the floor in front of Lizzie and reached for her hand. "I'm sorry." Those two words were more a shallow attempt to assuage my guilt than a true effort to comfort her. "I never meant to doubt you. I didn't know."

Whatever darkness had consumed Lizzie slowly faded, her eyes blinking rapidly before she crawled out of Seamus's embrace and took in the room. Her eyes landed on Liam. He had kicked the axe handle out of her reach and was slowly prying the metal head from Mr. Borden's skull.

"Leave it," she said.

"We can't," Liam replied as he slowly rocked the axe head back and forth until it popped free. "Bridget, you need to go. Right now. They will blame this on you."

"No. They won't." Lizzie fired back. "I will protect her, you have my word."

"Ah, lass, your word means very little to me," Liam said as he tossed the head of the axe next to its mangled handle. Ignoring Lizzie, he turned his attention to me. "Come now, love. Seamus and I will speak to the fact that you were in my flat with me all morning and nowhere near here."

"No," I said and stood up. "I won't leave Lizzie here alone. She will hang for this just as clearly as I would. I won't let that happen."

"Difference is, *she* actually did kill him," Seamus said.

The sarcasm I could hear in his voice pitched my anger to a new level, and I nearly lashed out at him. "What are you doing here, anyway? How did you even know to come?"

"Eli Bence," Seamus said, and both Lizzie and I swung our heads in his direction. "I stopped by the pharmacy on my way to the iron works. I wanted to check and see how his brother was faring. He told me about the . . . ah . . . purchase Lizzie tried to make and that he hadn't seen you in a few days. Liam had mentioned that you weren't feeling well, so . . ."

"So you assumed I had poisoned her?" The shock in Lizzie's voice was pure, filled less with anger than remorse. "I would never. Bridget means more to me than my own sister. I did this for her," she said sweeping her hand out in her father's direction, "to keep her safe and free from speculation."

Her eyes traveled down to the pool of blood beneath her feet. "He would have seen her hung for this. My father would have stopped at nothing until she was ruined." The words were no more than a hushed whisper, but I heard the truth lingering beneath them. Lizzie cared, would rather see herself jailed than me.

And Liam and Seamus just expected me to leave her here, coated in her father's blood, exposed to whatever story this city, these people, wanted to dream up.

I watched in horrified silence as Liam picked up the head of the broken axe and silently strode from the room. Seamus just shrugged, as if he was torn between following his brother and physically picking me up and dragging me with them. He knew better than to do the latter. No matter where they took me or how hard they tried to keep me close, I'd be back in an hour, a week, a month, to stand by Lizzie's side.

The door to the cookstove slammed shut, the smell of mutton stew permeating the air. "Give me your clothes," Liam said with a resigned sigh. His hands were covered in ash, the blade of the axe now as black as the night sky. "I'll burn them in the furnace at the mill."

I ran up the back staircase and fetched Lizzie a new dress, brought it down to her along with a few extra pins for her hair. I prayed her undergarments were unsoiled. The clean ones were still hanging on the line to dry, and I didn't want to risk being seen as I pulled them in.

She was down to her corset by the time I returned. Liam was seven shades of red, Seamus as calm as anything. She gave Liam her dress, and he handed her a rag from the kitchen, motioning for her to clean the blood from her face and hands.

"Don't open the stove," Liam said as he leaned in to give me a kiss. "The handle to the axe is in there, and it will take a good hour for it to burn clean through. The head won't burn but the ash should take care of any blood. I'll throw it in the barn on my way out."

I nodded and headed into the kitchen, where I tossed an onion and an entire jar of dried pepper into the stew, to cover up the scent of burning wood.

"Listen to me, Bridget," he said as he pulled me into his arms. "Seamus and I are going to leave. I want you to count to one hundred, then you and Lizzie are going to run out that front door, screaming as loud as you can. Carry on about a prowler and stumbling upon the Bordens' dead bodies. Get the police, the doctor, anybody who will listen, and tell them that neither you nor Lizzie saw anything. Got it?"

"Yes," Lizzie said from behind me.

"And you," Liam continued, refocusing on his brother. "You're going to take that off."

Seamus looked down and nodded, then proceeded to strip down to the yellowing undershirt he had on beneath. I hadn't noticed that Seamus's shirt was covered in blood, but Liam was right. An Irish boy covered in blood walking around Corky Row might not warrant calling the police, but it surely would here.

Liam locked eyes with me, then pursed his lips into a tight line. "It's going to be all right, you hear me? Just do exactly as I say, and it'll be fine. You have my word."

I stood there by the back door and watched them leave. Lizzie was counting quietly beside me, her gaze focused on Liam's disappearing figure. "You ready?" she asked.

I shook my head, then ran straight out the front door with Lizzie by my side.

Chapter 40

It seemed as though the entire town was lurking in the streets, hoping, waiting, for one of us to pull back the curtains so they could get a peek inside. Emma had yet to arrive home, but Alice was upstairs tending to Lizzie. Dr. Bowen had given Lizzie a tranquilizer, something to calm her nerves, or so he said. Funny how he didn't offer me anything, not that I would have taken it.

It had been nearly midday by the time the first police officer arrived. He took one look at Mr. Borden's body and ran for the back door and proceeded to vomit for a good five minutes, before he composed himself enough to run to the station and inform the marshal what had happened.

By the time they returned, Alice, Dr. Bowen, even nosy Mrs. Churchill had trampled through the house. I thought it was sacrilege, the way Lizzie just let anybody who wanted to walk through the house, staring and poking at her parents' dead bodies. I thought privacy would be more prudent, leaving fewer people to have to retell our story to. She laughed and told me this was better; any evidence Liam or Seamus had forgotten to clean up would be trampled out by the dozens of people traipsing in and out.

It was hours before they removed the bodies from the guest room and sitting room, and even then, they decided to toss them on the dining room table, cut them open, and empty the contents of their stomachs into jars. They took what was left of the stew and some milk as well, but not once did they think to open the cookstove, not once did they question the small smudge of ash on the kitchen floor.

"Bridget?" I turned at the sound of Mr. Morse's voice. He hadn't spoken to me since returning home that afternoon to find Dr. Bowen and the police surveying the bodies. In fact, he hadn't talked to anybody. He'd shown up shortly after the bodies had been moved to the dining room. He hadn't even entered the house, just cast a glance at Lizzie and then took a seat underneath the pear tree in the backyard. He'd reached up, picked a ripe piece of fruit from the tree, and bitten into it as if all this commotion were nothing more than a temporary inconvenience.

"Can I fix you something to eat?" I asked nervously. I poked around the ashes of the cookstove, moving the one tiny remaining piece of the axe handle into the center before restarting the fire. "Lizzie doesn't seem to have much of an appetite this evening, so I didn't prepare a meal, but it will only—"

He held up his hand, cutting me off. "No, I am fine."

"I'm sorry about Mr. Borden. I know you and him were close."

"Close?" he said, pausing as if considering the word. "Perhaps, but not for the reasons you may suspect."

I shrugged. I had learned this morning not to question anything when it came to this family. "Will you be in need of anything before I retire, sir?"

"Yes," he said and motioned for me to sit down. "Alice has agreed to stay the night, so Lizzie won't be alone. I would understand if you felt more comfortable somewhere else, and I'd be happy to make the necessary arrangements or escort you there myself."

I shook my head. "No, sir. I promised Lizzie I would stay."

"I know," he said as he took a seat across from me. He pulled a small envelope from his coat pocket and laid it on the table. When

I failed to inquire about it, he slid it in my direction. "I spoke with Lizzie. I know what happened today."

I stared at the envelope. Seamus's last words to me before he left were to say as little as possible to as few people as I could. I did as he'd instructed and stayed silent.

Mr. Morse tapped the envelope and went on. "Lizzie made me promise to steer the investigation away from you regardless of what it costs her. I don't think it wise, she is my niece after all, but I will honor her wishes."

I nodded, acknowledging nothing.

"Once this incident runs its course, I want you to leave, return to Ireland, and never come back to this city."

I watched as he pulled open the envelope and placed a stack of money on the table. It was more cash than I'd ever seen. More than I could even fathom. "This is the money Lizzie spoke with you about. Her proceeds from the sale of the house on Ferry Street. I'll take care of your passage personally, but this should help you start over."

I didn't need anybody to buy my silence. I wouldn't turn on Lizzie. I'd already vowed to her and to God that I would never breathe a word of what had really happened in this house.

"I don't want your money, sir."

"It's not his. It's mine," Lizzie said. I hadn't heard her come down the back stairs, hadn't known she was listening. "And I need you to take it. I owe you that and more for the friendship you have offered me. Take it. For you and Liam. For Cara."

Lizzie drew closer and collected the money from the table. She tucked it deep into the envelope and then pressed it into my palm. "Please."

Just as I'd been caught off-guard by her tears, so was I by her begging. Lizzie never begged anyone for anything, let alone gave away money when it seemed that was all she ever wanted. Then again, I'd been blind to more than the true Lizzie for a long time.

Andrew Borden was more than a miser; he was a madman. And Abigail Borden wasn't the frail, feeble-minded woman I always presumed. But John Morse . . . to me, he is still the mysterious brother of Lizzie's long-dead mother, the strange, uninvited guest who, to this day, I still can't quite figure out.

Epilogue

It's always the same. The click of my boots echoing off the hardwood floors. The light streaming in through the dingy, lace curtains. The smells drift back into my nose, thick and deathly, and for whatever reason, I am climbing the stairs. They moan beneath my feet, and I pause as the clock in the parlor sounds, warning me.

I'm halfway up the stairs now, and I can see them. Mrs. Borden's shoes. They stick out at a strange angle, what little bit of leather I can make out streaked in blood. I turn to scream, to escape down the stairwell that seems to be closing in on me, but find myself face to face with Andrew Borden. His flesh is rotting, falling in strips from his battered skull. His eyes are those of the dead pigeons, black and staring at me, daring me to tell the truth.

"Wake up, love."

I startle awake. The blankets are twisted around my body, and I'm drenched in sweat. My body shivers as the cool night air filters in through the open window. No matter how many miles I put between me and Fall River, no matter how many years pass, the dream never changes. The memories never fade.

Liam gets up, and I know he's going to close the window. We have this argument every time he wakes me in the throes of a nightmare, my body inconceivably cold.

"Leave it," I beg. The windows in that house were always closed, locking the darkness inside. Here they are always open, the cool, untainted air filtering through the house. *My* house.

"All right, lass," he says as he settles in next to me and drags my still-shaking body into his arms. His strong hand wraps around my shoulder, his wedding band shining in the early morning sun. "You're safe here with me and Cara." He breathes out, tightening his grip and dropping a kiss to my forehead.

Cara. I stare out the window, focusing on the mountains in the distance, to remind myself of how far I truly am from Fall River. From the smell of the river and the steam from the streetcars. From rancid meat and gossiping shopkeepers. From Lizzie Borden. And yet, I can never quite purge myself of it. I can never completely lose the dark bits that seem to tarnish me.

"I'm going to go wash up," Liam smiles, the bright blue of his eyes reminding me of that very first day we met.

I slip my night coat on and move into the hall, hovering outside Cara's door. She's still asleep, the gentle rise and fall of her chest telling me she's in a peaceful place. It took us months to get her here. There was the trial and then the journey back to Ireland. We'd also needed time to buy my parents a new farm and get them settled, followed by what seemed like an eternity of searching for somewhere we would fit in. Somewhere the news of Fall River's murderous spinster had not reached. Somewhere the name Lizzie Borden meant nothing.

Searching for some warmth, I slip my hand into the pocket of my night coat, my fingers curling around the envelope. The letter came over a month ago, and I've yet to open it.

The handwriting on the front is distinctive and the postmark is from an address in Fall River that I know well—a sizeable mansion with room for a dozen families. When Liam first handed it to me, I could smell the jasmine lingering on the thick, white paper. Now, after weeks of sitting unopened in my pocket, it bears the faintest hint of mountain air.

I feel Liam's warm breath on my neck, his hands tangling around my waist. "She's happy now, Bridget. She's got the house she always wanted on the Hill. She's got servants, a coachman . . . she's even got another maid."

Another maid. The words pierce my heart. True, she's got another maid, but if my instincts are right, she hasn't got another friend. According to the newspapers, Lizzie is a free woman. Free to live on the Hill. Free to entertain whomever she likes and to live the life she's always wanted. But I can't shake the feeling that as lonely as her life was when I lived there, it's worse now.

Liam pulls me in close and kisses me once more, before moving towards the kitchen and the chatter I can hear building behind the door. Saturday is the only day all four of us have off from work, and Seamus and Minnie are already awake. If I don't get myself straightened out, they'll tear apart the kitchen looking for food.

I pull on a dress and draw my hair up into a tight bun. Opening the door into the kitchen, I see Seamus laughing over a cup of coffee. Minnie is tucked close into his side. The grin on her face stretches wide as he leans over to kiss her, and I can't help but smile myself.

Seamus locks eyes with me and gives a tight nod. No doubt he faces the same set of dark feelings each morning, the same cycle of nightmares each night. But if he had to do it all over again, if he had to stand by Liam, by me, and by Lizzie, I know he would. We all would. It was the only way.

About the Authors

Trisha Leaver lives on Cape Cod with her husband, three children, and one rather irreverent black lab. She is a chronic daydreamer who prefers the cozy confines of her own imagination to the mundane routine of everyday life. To learn more about Trisha's books, her upcoming shenanigans, and her quest to reel in the perfect tuna, please visit her website at: *www.trishaleaver.com.*

Lindsay Currie is the coauthor of *Creed* and *Hardwired* as well as the author of the young adult contemporary novel *Jammed.* She lives in Chicago, Illinois, with one incredibly patient hubby, three amazing kids, and one adorable, but irreverent, bullmastiff named Sam. She's fond of coffee, chocolate, and things that go bump in the night. Learn more about her at *http://lindsaycurrie.com.*